Protect Me

KATIE CROSS

KCW

Chapter One

KATELYN

A pair of glaring red lights jerked in front of my car, nearly clipping my front bumper.

Reflexively, I stomped on my brakes. My car skidded to a stop seconds before it would have slammed into an obnoxiously lifted truck with chrome rims.

"Jerk face!" Knuckles white on the steering wheel, I loosened my clenched jaw. "May you get fined and not be able to pay the bill, you arrogant, slimy newt!"

A hitch the size of Kansas would have totaled my front end.

Not that it mattered.

With a belch of black smoke, the truck scampered down the mountain highway, the driver oblivious.

The ring of my phone echoed through my car, distracting me from my rage. With a deep exhale, I hit the *accept* button on my car dashboard.

The dulcet tone of my best friend, Vinita, followed.

"Kaaaaaatelyn!"

"Hey," I breathed, relieved to hear her voice. "Please tell me something happy about you and Zayne. How are baby preparations going?"

Concern laced her tone. "Uh oh. What's going on?"

My nostrils flared as I hesitated to respond. Vinita was only a few short months away from delivering her first baby—a boy. Not being at her side during this momentous time was hard enough, but the breakdown of my day made everything worse.

"Talk to me," Vinita commanded when my silence continued. Realizing I wouldn't be able to squirrel out of it, I gave in.

"It's just . . . today was the worst day ever. I dropped three drinks at work this morning, the espresso machine stopped working, Dahlia called in sick so I had to do the morning rush myself and I still don't know the drinks super well. It took me forever to do anything, so the line built up. People got all passive-aggressive and huffy. To make it worse . . . " I sighed. ". . . last night, I couldn't get any sleep."

The hastily-stated final sentence was a bald lie.

Sort of.

I couldn't get any sleep was code for *the nightmares are coming back.* Vinita and I always had our own language.

"Again?" she asked softly.

Tears filled my eyes at her compassionate tone, but I blinked them back. "Yeah, but it's fine." I cleared my throat. "Really."

"Kaaaaaatelyn!"

The sharp edge of her reprimand made me laugh—she sounded just like her mother, Vani.

"I'm fine, really." A sniffle punctuated my insistence. I pulled off the side of the road, chest heavy. "I just . . . I don't know what triggered the nightmares this time, but I'll figure it out and work through it. It's been a year since I last had a dream like that. I kind of hoped I was over it already."

"You don't just *get over* trauma like that."

I snorted. "Don't I know that. Maybe healing never ends?"

"Of course it does. It's been five years, Kate. Look how far you've come. You've worked so hard in therapy, but that doesn't mean healing is absolute or even linear. You'll slip back into memories every now and then and you'll fight your way back to the light. I'm here for you."

Having a Marriage and Family Therapist as a best friend had been a lifesaver for *so* many reasons.

I swallowed again. "I know. Thank you for the reminder. So, what's up?"

Sighing, she said, "I had a favor to ask, but now I realize it may not be the best time."

"No! Give me the favor." My hands flapped with my insistence. "Give me something that I can do to help you. I can't be in New York with you and your baby and it's *killing me* to be this far apart."

"I know!" she wailed. "I've missed you so much. Once the baby is born, Zayne will fly you out to visit. Anyway, Amma will be staying with me for over a month after the birth, so I'll need your help to keep me from going crazy from all her fussing over me. Within a week, you'll be so tired of living with me, you'll wish to be back there."

"Never!"

"I love hearing that," she cried. "Anyway, something is wrong with Vikram and we need your help. Amma is a mess."

My wrung-out heart twisted at the sound of her older brother's name. It resounded like a dull echo in my brain.

Vikram, the hero of my childhood. The ruggedly dashing young man that became a wild adult. Vikram, the love of my life. The light in my dark teenage sky. The lover of women and carelessness and impulsivity. My breath came fast just thinking about him, the man I intentionally hadn't thought of in over five years.

The man I'd never have.

"Vikram?"

"We can't get a hold of him."

"Tell me more," I said quickly, because anything else would have been a gasp. When the mention of his name set my heart to racing, I knew I was in big trouble.

"He was supposed to have knee surgery a few days ago. Bastian was going to drive him home afterwards. Amma spoke to him right before, and he seemed fine. We haven't heard from him since then."

"You think he's okay?"

"I hope so, but he's not answering calls, emails, or text messages. Bastian's old number isn't working, and Grady has been on vacation with his wife for a while. I tried finding Hernandez's number, but I couldn't."

Stress tugged at her voice, making the vowels slightly longer than usual. I'd do anything that Vinita asked of me. We were sisters from the past. Our lives had combined in all ways as we grew up next door to each other, intertwining like fate meant to braid us together. Without Vinita and the safety of her family, there would be no Katelyn today.

"Do you want me to go to Vik's townhouse?" I asked.

Her voice elevated. "Would you mind?" Although still bright, I read the hesitation there. Vinita, of anyone, would understand my hesitation. I clung to nine rules for life and ultimate safety.

1. Never alone.
2. Never in the dark.
3. Always lock the door.
4. Don't go anywhere new by myself.
5. Never speak about what happened.
6. Never talk about my aunt.
7. Don't go on a date without someone else knowing every detail.
8. Don't share name identifiers, my email, or phone number with strangers.
9. Never unaware.

In the last five years, the rules never failed to keep me safe. I'd applied them to every situation, job interview, apartment application, friend, and had never strayed once from the boundaries.

So far, safe.

Going to Vikram's apartment meant I'd need to go alone. Sure, I could bring a friend, but Vikram wouldn't open the door. Although I hadn't seen him in over five years, even I knew that.

Vikram of the last year was . . . lost. He dwindled, alone, while his best friends advanced into their lives with new girlfriends or wives. Commitment-phobe Vik probably couldn't process why they would attach themselves to another human so concretely.

Based on what Amma relayed to me, anyway.

If any man was safe enough to break my iron-clad rules, Vikram would be the *only* one. Like me, he'd remained in the Pineville area after high school, though his parents and sister moved away. A train conductor when it suited him, a ladies' man without promises, and a freeball adventurer the rest of the time, he commanded life.

Until life handed him an empty bowl of loneliness after his friends paired off with girlfriends or wives. A recent knee injury while dog sledding in the arctic sure didn't help things.

"I wouldn't mind checking on him at all," I said, and managed to mean it.

"Really?" she drawled.

"Really."

"Listen," her voice softened, "you know you're safe with Vik, right? That he wouldn't . . . I mean you grew up with him. He thinks of you like a little sister. At least, he used to. You know, when he came home more often and didn't try to shut the world out all the time."

A heavy lump rose in my throat, but I swallowed it back. "Yes, I know."

"Still, if you don't—"

"It's fine, Vinita. Really. I'm happy to help however I can, especially with you so far away. Being near your brother will be the next best thing to being close to you."

"I miss you," Vinita said. "I wish you could be here for the birth of the baby."

"Me too."

The amusement in her voice warmed me. Vinita and Vikram had been raised in the US, but kept ties with their family members in South India all their life. Now, Vinita lived in upper New York State with her husband Zayne in an adorable house with a white picket fence nestled in a neighborhood. She would have her son without me there to welcome him to the world.

It stung, but what could be done?

No money, no flight.

"I'll go check on him now," I said. "I just got off work and . . . don't really have anything to fill the rest of my day."

"You are the best!" she cried, and the relief in her voice made everything worth it. "Thank you, Kate. I'll text you as soon as I hang up. Let me know what happens okay?"

I'll fall in love with him all over again, I thought. *That's what will happen. I'll fall in love for a second time with the one man that I love, hate, and can't have.*

"Of course. Talk to you soon."

I ended the call and stared straight ahead with the sinking feeling that I'd just altered the course of the rest of my life.

* * *

Vikram's townhouse on the outer limits of Pineville was only a few minutes from where I worked at the Frolicking Moose Coffee Shop. The short drive still provided ample time for me to think out every possible way this visit could go wrong.

Like the time when, as an awkward twelve-year-old, I had

dumped tomato soup on his shirt when we ran into each other in the kitchen.

Or the time he brought a date home, smacked lips with her on the couch, and I caught them in a . . . compromising position . . . with a flip of the light. That wouldn't have been so bad, but Amma had trailed in behind me.

Vikram had been grounded for weeks.

With memories like those to accompany me, I grimaced the whole drive.

Since I moved into my aunt's house at ten years old, Vik had had the uncanny ability to turn me into a blundering mess. His quick smile melted my stomach to lava. The sound of his voice as he chattered with Appa made my heart flutter. Around Vikram, I lived like a heart attack victim.

Annoyed, I turned off the highway.

"I'm not twelve anymore," I said firmly. "Vikram is a friend now. Like a brother, that's all."

I pointedly ignored the fact that I knew where he lived, though I hadn't spoken to him in . . . years? I tried not to count.

Okay, fine.

Four years, eleven months, and three weeks.

By the time I parked and walked up to his apartment, my blood smoked. Heart sprinted. Lungs felt short and compressed. Thoughts of Vinita propelled me forward. A tizzy of breathlessness of this proportion was ridiculous. For all I knew, Vikram wouldn't even open the door.

I'd be lucky if he spoke *through* it, honestly.

Gathering the last of my courage, I rapped with my knuckles and ignored the urge to duck out of sight of the peephole. That would guarantee that he wouldn't open the door.

No answer.

"Vik?" I called.

My voice croaked. Some people carried their emotions in

their eyes, but mine lived in my words. The way they quivered, turned cold as ice, or warm as tea.

Now?

I sounded like a bullfrog.

With a little quiver, I cleared my throat and knocked again. "I know you're inside. Vini just called me. Let me in?"

The plea went unanswered. I strained to hear any sound, but none came. I chewed on my bottom lip. The concern in Vini's voice had been real enough and she had better things to worry about than her selfish, ridiculous brother. Namely, growing her firstborn, my nephew.

Indignation on behalf of Vinita flushed through me. If anything would give me courage and power, my loyalty to Vinita was *the* thing. A stroke of inspiration rippled through me.

With my fist, I banged.

"Vikram Ramesh Manav—"

The door flew open.

I stopped, strangled by surprise. Two dark, slitted eyes glared at me. When a flash of bare, muscular shoulders caught my dropping gaze, I jerked my eyes back to his. Sweet baby pineapple, as Lizbeth would say.

Vikram wasn't wearing a shirt.

From what I could tell, he wore a pair of baggy gray sweats, cut off at the knee on the right side. Crutches braced his body. The desire to check his feet—they'd be bare because he had always hated shoes—almost urged me to look down again.

Instead, I kept my gaze high and steady.

Nope.

Couldn't ogle Vik.

Drawn back by something more than sheer desire, I glanced to his right knee. A bulky wrap covered the brown skin there, an ugly interruption to firm legs. Quick as a shot, I looked back to his eyes in silent uncertainty.

He studied me, stony as a statue.

Vikram hated nothing more than his long name—poetically beautiful, if you asked me—but the embarrassment of his childhood. Bastian and Grady had teased him relentlessly over all seven names given to him by his exuberant, loving mother. He never wanted anyone to know them. Calling the first three out now had been a lucky guess.

Nostrils flared, he uttered three hard words.

"Low blow, Kate."

His voice shocked life back into my veins. How long had it been since I'd heard my name on his lips? Too long. The sound used to trigger my teenage daydreams. Not even the condemnation and annoyance in his words could bother me.

Vikram had *spoken*.

"Can I come in?"

Five long seconds passed. Just as I prepared myself to lift an arm and block him from slamming the door in my face, he huffed.

"Fine."

Chapter Two

VIKRAM

Katelyn Saucony, the last person I would have expected on my doorstep.

Well.

I'll be damned.

In hindsight, I should have anticipated such a twisted move. Vinita had a hand as meddling as my mother's. She'd always been a better chess player, too. Kingslayer, I used to call Vini. One day, she'd pay for this.

For now, I needed to sit down.

Katelyn eyed me like a wary cat when I shuffled back, crutches painful under my arms, and left the door open for her to close. The world tipped whenever I stood, but I tried to hide the drunken feeling. Heaven knew, I'd experienced it enough. Just like the pained grimace I bit back by sheer willpower.

I'd brought this on myself.

A few moments later, I sank back onto the couch. Was there an imprint from my body here yet? Too late to check, I'd already closed my eyes. The ethereal, hazy quality of the world returned. If I didn't need these painkillers so much to function, I'd tie them to an 80 pound weight, throw them into the deepest reaches of the ocean, and wave goodbye.

Wait, what was happening?

My eyes opened, latching onto Kate again.

Right, Katelyn.

I needed to get off this medicine.

"Tell Vini I'm fine," I muttered. Did I imagine the slur in my voice? What I didn't dream was the way Katelyn fidgeted with the bottom of her shirt. Her top teeth worried her bottom lip, blanching the plush skin there. I tilted my head back to help my eyes close faster, but they opened again.

Why was she still so nervous around me?

"You had surgery," she said, a bit unnecessarily. Her eyes darted back to my knee.

I swallowed, my throat dry as Hades.

What response could she possibly expect?

"Yes."

"Are you . . . all right?"

"No."

A rustling sound followed. I cracked one eye to see her bent over the couch, picking up a wrapper between two fingers. She stopped, gazed around the littered mess of my townhouse. Her eyebrows pulled together.

To her credit, she let no disgust show on her face—though I wouldn't have blamed her. I hadn't cleaned up after myself in several days. Wrappers, old water bottles, and empty medicine bottles cluttered the ground. I'd shuffled around with my crutches, making trails out of the wreckage. Somewhere in the chaos waited a garbage bag, but it might be under a pile of blankets by now.

Had that been before or after the fever?

Katelyn opened her mouth, then closed it again. She pivoted on the spot, and her twirl sent my head spinning. I closed my eyes to make it stop. One long blink later, a *shuck* of sound drew me back to the land of the living.

My apartment had transformed.

No more wrappers, bottles, or garbage could be found. Kate had just dumped a bunch of clothes into a pile on the couch nearby, and the sound had been her shaking a blanket. Her arms paused. She turned, looked right at me. Her eyes widened. She covered her mouth with a hand.

"So sorry. Did I wake you?" she whispered.

Unconsciousness beckoned.

I answered.

* * *

Wakefulness returned in gentle waves.

First, I heard a low murmur. A woman. Simone, from next door? No, someone else. The tones were expressive, though hushed. The more I focused, the more the sound turned into words. My head cleared.

"No, Vini. He's just . . . out of it. I called the number on some discharge paperwork and I'm waiting for his doctor to call me back. No. I don't think he needs 911. I mean, I don't know? He's breathing. Color seems okay."

Vini.

Discharge paperwork.

Fuuuudgesicle.

Regret and a low thrum of frustration washed through me. The pain pills had cleared out of my mind, but so had their numbing effect. My knee ached like a hot poker was stuck under the skin. The pain flared into my ankle and hip like flames. With the agony came clarity. Clarity, I'd take.

Unless it illuminated . . .

Katelyn.

Infection.

My sister and her meddling, Kingslayer ways.

Suppressing a groan, I opened my eyes. Kate stood at the island in my kitchen right across from me. The counters sparkled. Crumbs, wrappers, and dirty dishes had been cleared away. The windows were thrown open, admitting a clean breeze that felt like heaven.

Had she cleaned the glass?

Sunlight sparkled as it slanted inside. A hint of bleach lay in the air. The temptation to shove off the couch, spring to my feet, and demand she leave nearly overcame me. Reality cut down that idea a little *too* swiftly. I could no sooner climb to my feet than throw her out. How had I even made it to the door to answer it?

When had I let her in?

Memories were fragmented, unclear.

My hand snaked up to my forehead, feeling it. The fever from earlier had broken, at least. A shower was in order. I smelled ripe as days-old fish.

Could I shower?

I glanced at my knee next, unable to stop a wince. Though I couldn't see it now, I recalled the gaping wound with a shudder. Man, that thing was hideous. Bright red, like a tiger had clawed through me, then someone yanked the skin back together with black strings and hope. No nasty drainage was apparent through the bandages now, which I took for a good sign.

Small miracles.

"Yes," Katelyn murmured into the phone, "of course."

Slowly, I straightened up. How long had I been asleep? Judging by the cleanliness of my apartment—except for what lay right next to me—several hours. As if that hadn't been confounding enough, the second shock occurred to me next.

Katelyn Saucony in. my. apartment.

Wonders *never* ceased.

My gaze roved over her, the best friend of my little sister.

Quiet, wide-eyed, like a doe. She stood in profile, sunshine brightening her face, setting strands of light blonde hair on fire. It trailed around her shoulders, halfway to her elbow. She'd shoved her glasses into her hair, keeping it out of her eyes. Long sleeves had been pushed all the way up her arms, as if she'd *really* gotten into the act of cleaning my place. One of her arms was bent, the phone pressed to her ear.

"I'll stay," she said quietly. "I'll keep you updated. No, no, don't worry. Rules don't . . . those don't apply here."

My eyes fluttered closed again, on their own accord.

Rules?

Katelyn ended the call just as I opened my eyes again. She had glanced my way, almost errantly, then did a double take when she caught my gaze.

Her back straightened.

"Hey."

"Hey," I croaked.

"Feeling better?"

She stepped forward. Might have been the drugs twisting my memory, but she seemed a lot less frightened now than when she'd first arrived. Was frightened the right word? Taken aback, maybe?

Who wouldn't have been with me growling like a grizzly and smelling like this?

"Not sure," I murmured. "I think so."

She stopped in the doorway to the kitchen and leaned a shoulder against the door frame. Her arms folded across her chest.

"I, uh . . ."

"Thanks," I held up a hand to stop her. "Sorry if I was cranky. The meds they have me on are a bit of a trip."

Her stiff smile softened. She shrugged one shoulder. "No problem."

I drew in a breath, held it, and attempted to stand. The

expected pain came, but I breathed out, working through it. The dizziness followed, and that's what kept taking me down.

Katelyn materialized at my side.

"Let me help."

I had half a second to decide before I would fall back onto the couch and endure a shock of pain that would last minutes. That would be unbearable, so I gritted my teeth and accepted her offered shoulder. She braced herself, stabilizing me, with an arm around my waist. The heat of her arm was a welcome touch.

How long had it been since I'd *seen* another person?

"Thanks."

"I can take it," she said. "You can lean on me."

With hesitation, I let my hand rest on her other shoulder. She moved closer, allowing me to shift my weight onto her. Her shoulder tucked right under my arm, like a missing puzzle piece that had come together. My toes dug into the carpet as I solidified my stance, then reached for a crutch.

"Thanks."

Several seconds passed while I got my metaphorical—and literal—feet under me. She stood immovable at my side.

"Got it. I can walk, I just . . . I get dizzy." Despite myself, I couldn't help a wry smile down at her. "Guess it's been awhile since you've experienced me without a shower or deodorant."

She chortled. "A very long while. If I remember right, you started wearing deodorant in elementary school."

"I did. You remember that?"

Her cheeks brightened in a little blush. She kept her gaze down.

"Lucky guess."

Liar.

If Vinita had been the Kingslayer, then Katelyn had been the Eternal Second. Always at Vinita's side. The quiet voice of reason, diplomacy, and logic. The quiet of *everything*. Katelyn crept around my memories like a fog, a whisper, a dream. A will-o'-wisp come to life that fluttered around the calmest parts.

There, but gently so.

She never wanted to draw attention to herself, but couldn't stay away. The moth to Vinita's flame. They'd been inseparable in my memories, too. I hardly pictured my sister without thinking of Katelyn.

Even if barely.

Her big eyes peered at me, unreadable. Katelyn had always been carefully distant. Amma, Appa, Vinita, they could touch her. They were openly affectionate, like Amma and Appa would be with me and Vini. But there had always been a firm wall between us. After Vinita and Katelyn graduated high school together, Katelyn had disappeared into thin air. She popped up only at family functions.

Or was that me?

"Just need to go to the bathroom." I licked my lips, suddenly out of words. "And take a shower."

"Are you allowed to?" She eyed my bandage. "That seems pretty fresh."

"I'll be careful."

Regardless, I had to get clean. With a detachable showerhead and a lot of towels, I could make this happen.

"Sure," she drawled.

"It's down the hall."

"I know." The color on her face deepened, but she met my gaze this time. "I cleaned it."

My nose wrinkled. "You survived?"

She laughed, a quiet trill. The sound seemed to take both of us by surprise. "Yes, and lived to tell the tale."

"I'm sorry."

"Don't be. How long have you been . . . ah . . ."

"A troll?"

She pursed her lips together to stop a smile. "I was going to say *recovering*."

We moved forward as a unit, down the hallway. My head stopped slipping out from beneath me, and the movement became less concerning. Once we made it to the hall, I reached a hand out to stabilize and take some of my weight back. She eyed it, said nothing.

"Did Vini send you?" I asked in a blatant misdirection of her question.

"Yes."

I scowled. "Kingslayer."

She laughed, and the delight that echoed in it slipped all the way through me like a bolt of lightning. The fog that caused everything to haze over cleared, and I realized just how terrible and lonely all of this must appear.

She paused outside the bathroom.

"Do you need—"

I held up a hand. "I got this."

"Right. I'll just . . ." She hooked a thumb over her shoulder, blush intensifying. "I'll just be out . . . there."

Katelyn spun on her heel and scuttled away before I could say another word.

KATELYN

My heart hammered like a wild thing.

The sound of the running shower reassured me that he couldn't hear my erratic pulse, but I wasn't totally convinced. Blood rushed through my ears and my breath fluttered with every inhale and exhale. I paced across the kitchen floor, body racing.

Sweet baby pineapple.

Vikram.

Vikram.

Vikram.

Everything I'd once admired about him as a young, love-struck girl had only intensified with time. The rugged beauty. The occasional jaded malevolence. Vikram didn't just walk into a room, he *owned* the room—and the people in it.

On his own, with a nasty scar and a brooding temperament —riddled with flashes of charm—and he still had my heart. My soul. He gripped them in his fingers, tangling my heartstrings as he tugged them along.

The man still looked like an Indian god come to life with his dark eyes and swept-back hair. Bedraggled, he still managed to look sexy. I pressed my hand to my forehead and let out a long breath.

"Get it together, Kate," I hissed. "You survived Aunt Trina, you can survive this. Get him settled, make him dinner, and get out of here. Rule number one. Never alone."

A scoff rolled out of me.

No, I had no fear over Vikram.

He was weak as a kitten, though he tried to hide it. He couldn't hurt me if he tried. Not physically, and I'd never give any man a reason for power over me in *any* form. The reality of his situation, and my deep loyalty to Vinita, brought my resolve to be helpful back. A new plan formed.

Once Vikram returned from his shower, I'd help him get settled. I'd cobble together a grocery list, prep a few meals, and promise to check on him in a day or two. He seemed lucid enough now.

Space and time.

If we have nothing else, Vinita always reminded me when she slipped into therapist mode, *our hearts heal with space and time.*

My heart didn't need to heal.

It needed to find all the lost pieces first.

* * *

Vikram stumbled out of the bathroom half an hour later. Only when I saw his pale face and drawn expression did I feel a stab of fear.

Should I have helped him?

Recovery from getting sliced open was hardly my forte. When possible, I avoided blood, gore, and anything associated with pain. Hospitals sent a deathly shiver through me.

"You don't look so good," I said, already at his side.

He smiled grimly, knuckles white on his crutches. The

muscles of his forearms flexed, too defined by half. There was no reason to be this perfect.

"Peachy," he muttered.

Okay, right.

I deserved that.

"Can I help you back to the couch?"

His nostrils flared. "Sure."

I followed at his side, annoyed by the regret that he'd donned an old shirt. A second pair of chopped sweatpants, these black, covered his legs.

While he showered, I'd cleaned up the couch, removed the dirty blankets and pillows, replaced them with new ones, and put more clothes in the laundry. The coffee table had been littered with pill bottles, glasses of water, and boxes of half-eaten food. I'd cleared it off and then filled water bottles to stash in the fridge.

As we approached, his gaze roved over the clean area with glazed surprise. He paused at the coffee table, then glanced to the right, near the kitchen.

"Mind if we detour? I'm so sick of this view."

"Sure."

"Are you going to stay?"

"Yes?"

He eyed me. I met the challenge in his stare. Old Katelyn would have cowered. Dropped his gaze, fumbled for a reply.

I wasn't that girl anymore.

"Do you want me to?" I asked.

He grumbled. "Sure."

"Then I'll stay."

He settled at the table, blinking as if he still was coming out of a haze. Micro grimaces appeared in the twitch of his lips, a ruffle of nose. My stomach clenched, more affected by his pain than I wanted to admit.

When he broke his arm in middle school, he'd walked

around for days with his teeth clenched. I felt sick to my stomach the whole time. Vinita and I had stayed far away while he prowled around, surly and snappish. He never frightened me, but I hated the agony in his expression. Couldn't stand the thought of not fixing his broken parts.

Unsure of what to do next, I headed back to the sink.

"So," he drawled, sounding so much like the Vikram I once knew that it turned my blood cold. "Vinita sent you."

I kept my back to him.

"She's worried."

"I didn't know you were in the area."

"I moved back to Pineville a few months ago."

"Didn't like Jackson City?"

I shrugged, "Kind of busy. Touristy. Wanted something a little more quiet."

And a little more mine, I silently added.

"I work at the coffee shop."

"You like it?"

"A lot."

I reached for a towel and grabbed a glass that was drying on the counter. Seemed easier not to address the deeper question there. The one that said *why would you live here?*

Or maybe it said something else.

"Thank you."

He said it so quietly I thought I might have imagined it. I paused, set the glass down, and turned to face him. He stared at me from beneath a heavy brow.

"Sure."

Before I turned back to the dishes—and tried to remember my plan to get out of here—he attempted to stand. In three steps, I stood in front of him, blocking his way.

"What do you need?"

He growled.

I stood my ground.

"I'm thirsty," he said. "I'm going to get some water."

"Let me do it."

"I'm not a child."

"No, you're a surly tiger." My hand touched his shoulder. "I've got it."

A spark raced through me. I spun so he didn't see the light race up my face in a bright blush. My mind settled on a memory. Summertime. A BBQ in their backyard where Vinita and I ran around in our swimsuits under the sprinklers. Water glinted under a hot, blue sky, and Vikram and his three friends—the Merry Idiots—lounged under the tree. They drank root beer, he had water. He laughed, throat bobbing, and I avoided him more than ever that day. He'd always brought me to life in new and unexpected ways.

How did time not erase such a thing?

My skin burned where the tip of my finger had rested on his shoulder. Years had passed since I'd willingly touched a man. I'd expected terror or fear or uncertainty. Instead, warmth flooded me.

Holy coconuts.

This was worse than I thought.

He nodded thanks as I passed him a water bottle from an almost-empty fridge. Only a baking soda box, an old carton of rice, and two eggs lay inside, next to a grouping of water bottles on the bottom shelf. I closed it, then glanced around.

"What are you looking for?" he asked.

"Paper. We're going to make a grocery list."

He opened his mouth to protest, but I shot him a glare to make Vinita proud. He held up a hand in defeat.

"Fine. Far drawer, near the stove."

Pen and paper in hand, I sat across from him and focused on the page, far from his too-intense glower. "Coconut milk, rice, coconut and cilantro for chutney, and eggs, obviously," I drawled. "What else?"

A beat of silence followed.

I glanced up to find him staring at me, appearing startled. He shook his head to clear it, rattled off a list of other things, none of which surprised me. Bags of frozen veggies. Tomatoes, onions, ginger, and garlic for pulav. Kale. Sprouted whole wheat bread. Cage-free eggs, brown, from the organic section. Frozen blueberries and purple cabbage and sparkling water.

When he finished, I capped the pen and set it aside. "Do you want something to eat now?"

His lips pressed. "I should, but I'm not that hungry."

"How about I go get some fresh fruit?" I said, scribbling a few more things on the list. "I'll cut it up and put it in a bowl, the way you like. The honeydew is to die for right now. Cold fruit will probably help settle your stomach, or something."

Vikram went still again. Warily, I looked up. He regarded me with a fresh round of uncertainty. I felt paralyzed under such a piercing look.

Had I said something wrong?

We held the gaze for so long, I came undone from the inside out. Finally, he licked his lips and nodded.

"Thanks. I love fresh fruit."

My breath felt shaky as I drew it in, long, slow, and deep, all the way to the bottom of my lungs, where it would flush out all this . . . weirdness. The trembling. The bright-eyed teenager that shrieked to life inside me. The one that vowed to love Vikram to her dying day.

Today, she'd been unleashed. She bounced around giddy and terrified and powerful. I shot to my feet.

Time to make my escape.

"Be back soon, thanks!"

Chapter Four

VIKRAM

Vinita's fiery voice shot through the phone the moment she answered my call. "Well," she drawled, sharp with beseeching, "look who's alive after all!"

"You have *got* to be kidding me, Vini."

"Bring it on, Vik," she cried. "I'm pregnant, stuck in my house, and haven't been able to yell at anyone for weeks because my husband is a sweet, sensitive soul. I'm ready for a fight."

The force of her words woke me up. Who was I kidding? I could no more stand up to my sister right now than I could go for a run.

Why did I call anyway?

Oh, right.

Because Vinita sent a ghost to check on me. A lovely, full-grown, in-the-flesh ghost that I'd tended to ignore but now couldn't. A ghost that knew me far too well. One that fluttered around quietly, upending my chosen life as a momentary recluse.

Tiger, Katelyn had said.

That fit.

Even tigers needed to retreat and lick their wounds, though.

"I tried calling," Vini continued. "Endlessly. Amma has called. Appa. You haven't picked up."

"My surgery had complications while I stayed overnight," I muttered, running a hand through my still-wet hair. It lay down on my shoulders now, cool against my slightly fevered skin. "I'm fine . . . sort of. There was too much swelling and I had to go back in before I lost my leg and then it got infected somehow. I've been spiking fevers and . . . whatever. I'm fine."

Her silence unnerved me.

Vini was the authoritative type. If she didn't like what you had to say, she'd interrupt. Talk over you. Bowl you down until you gave up. Unless you were Zayne or Katelyn, Vini didn't care what you thought.

Most people gave her a wide berth when she was in a fighting mood, but not me. Secretly, I thought she might have sent Katelyn to prod the sleeping tiger, so to speak. Vini needed an outlet for all her natural ire.

Sometimes, that outlet was me.

"Kate said you didn't look good when she arrived."

"I'm fine. The painkillers make me woozy and I must have taken some on an empty stomach."

A sigh of frustration issued through the phone. "She said that you were out of it and groggy. You basically passed out while talking to her."

"I fell asleep on the couch. That's hardly life or death."

"For hours."

My gaze darted to the clock.

Yeah, well, that seemed correct.

"Look, I'm fine. I have an appointment with the doctor tomorrow and the antibiotics are finally working. The fevers have calmed and the pain is starting to be more manageable, okay? Kate is at the grocery store right now getting me food."

"Oh. Good."

The pressure in her tone dwindled. I let out a breath of

relief. If Vini could chill out, she wouldn't sic Amma on my case. The last thing I needed was Amma showing up. A shudder slipped through me.

"Look, Vini," I tilted my head back. "Thanks for being concerned, but I'm fine. Don't get Katelyn feeling all obligated to take care of me or check on me."

"Katelyn? Are you kidding? She loves helping people."

I snorted. Yeah, she seemed *super* excited about being here. I opened my mouth to say that, but stopped. No, Katelyn hadn't been the meek character I remembered from growing up. The girl that haunted our house because she never wanted to return to her aunt's house.

This Katelyn had more of a spine.

Still a ghost, though.

"Besides," Vini continued, "you're practically her brother. And," she tacked on quietly, "it's good for her, too."

Whatever that meant. The shower and this call had already worn me out. Time for nap number 4,567. My body trembled a little—chills—as I leaned forward to rest my left elbow on my good knee. Grief, but I was weak as a baby. Could barely hold my phone.

"I'm going to sleep on the couch," I said. "Thanks for sending her."

"Be nice," she growled.

"I am."

"Love you, Vik."

"You, too."

My phone turned dark as I set it down. If it wouldn't have hurt so much, I would have laid my head down on the table and fallen right to sleep. Instead, I slowly made my way back into the living room.

After taking my next round of antibiotics, avoiding the narcotics and going for the anti-inflammatories, I had a cracker, lowered onto the couch, chugged a water bottle, and fell back into a deep sleep with Vinita's words ringing restlessly through my mind.

You're practically her brother.

* * *

Darkness woke me.

My eyes flew open and I sucked in a sharp breath, startled by the drastic change in scenery. I'd fallen asleep in the middle of the day. A blanket of black lay on the apartment, punctuated only by the gentle illumination of a few kitchen appliances. The clock on the wall betrayed the hour.

3:30 am.

Startled, I straightened. The fever I'd fallen asleep with had subsided, leaving me clammy. Some of the throbbing pain in my knee left mild irritation behind. Twinges of pain moved through my hips, sore from so little activity. By no means comfortable, but not so damn intense.

What day was it?

Memory served. Katelyn. Vinita. Had that been sometime around three in the afternoon? I couldn't remember.

A gentle breath, and a stir of sound, whipped my head to the right.

Through the shadows, I could just make out a lithe feminine form on the couch across from me. Blonde hair brightened the arm rest, draped over the edge and trailing down. Katelyn. She'd curled around a pillow, face slack in sleep. A blanket covered her shoulder, her wide, black glasses askew on her face.

I ran a hand over my cheek, recalling most of yesterday through a haze. A blanket dropped onto my lap when I moved. She must have covered me up. Was she worried? Guilt rushed through me as I remembered.

I'd sort of been a jerk.

A rummy, hopped-up-on-meds-and-fever jerk.

Slowly, I stood. The rush of dizziness didn't come, only a mild twinge of pain. I straightened, grateful to move. Katelyn didn't stir as I slipped by to relieve my aching bladder. By the time I came out of the bathroom, she hadn't moved.

The thought of her being in my apartment for twelve hours while I slept, totally unaware, should have disturbed me. Had it been anyone but Katelyn, I would have been royally pissed, but Katelyn was too unobtrusive.

I grabbed another water bottle from the fridge. Light cut into the darkness, brightening the kitchen. My hand paused halfway there.

She'd restocked everything.

Milk. Eggs. Veggies. All the ingredients for pulav. Next to the fridge lay a package—dosa mix. She must keep it stocked at her place, because Pineville didn't have any here. In a glass bowl on the top shelf waited cut up fruit with all my favorite melons. Honeydew, cantaloupe, watermelon. My mouth watered. Appetite returned for the first time.

Not a ghost, I realized.

An angel.

With my left arm, I grabbed the bowl of fruit and set it on the table. Foregoing a fork—I didn't want to wake her—I made a second trip back for my water bottle, then sat down at the table in the darkness. The cool fruit, sweet and fresh, slid down my hot throat. I fought back a groan.

Better than anything.

When I'd eaten almost half the bowl, I forced myself to slow. Retching would only irritate the wound, and I didn't want Doc Blaine to have any reason to send me back to the hospital. Speaking of, I had to figure out how to *get* to my appointment later today.

I shook that off.

A rideshare would be fine.

The sound of a quiet voice sounded like a cannon in the

night. "Vik?" My head lifted, back toward the living room. Katelyn's sleepy tone, like a rustled puppy, sent heat all the way to my toes. I shoved it back.

Kate was practically my sister.

Right?

Didn't explain why her crackly voice made my fingers curl into fists I couldn't have unclenched if I tried.

"Yeah. Sorry if I woke you."

She darted up, eyes wild. Her hair flopped around her face and breaths came fast. I leaned back in the kitchen chair. Did I comprehend this wrong because of shadows, or was she in an outright panic?

"Kate?"

She sucked in a sharp breath. "Where am I?" Her knees curled into her chest. "I—"

"You're at my place." My voice dropped a notch, right into soothing. "In Pineville. I . . . I guess I fell asleep for a long time and you must have stayed to take care of me. Thank you."

The terror ebbed. The tight muscles in her face eased and shoulders slumped.

"Right. Sorry. I . . . sorry."

I grabbed the bowl of fruit and held it out to her. "Fruit makes everything better. Want some?"

Doubtful she could see more than my silhouette right now. I couldn't blame her for a momentary freak out with my ugly mug in the shadows, but I couldn't shake the feeling there was *more* to it than that.

Kate shoved the hair out of her face and behind an ear. Her death grip on her knees faded.

"Can I turn on a light?"

The request, so quietly spoken, cut to a heart I thought more hardened than this.

"Of course."

"Thanks."

A rustle, then a flicker of low light from a lamp. She didn't quite meet my eyes as she looked around—again—and finally settled back against the couch. Several moments passed before I shoved the bowl and fork away with my left hand.

"I owe you an apology."

Her head lifted. "What?"

"I was sort of a jerk earlier. I blame the meds." My fingers ran through my hair, tangled in the still-wet strands at the very back, where I'd been sleeping for hours. "There's . . . a lot going on."

"Oh, I didn't think you were a jerk."

"You should have."

"I didn't." She set her chin on top of her knees and sighed. "I didn't want to wake you and wasn't sure if you were okay, so I stayed. I hope—"

"It's fine. Appreciated, even. You went above and beyond what you needed to do. I'm all right, whether or not you can believe that."

The doubt in her gaze didn't surprise me. Maybe I *wasn't* fine, but I was at least put-together enough to acknowledge that much.

Hopefully, it meant something.

"Your doctor's office called me back." She clutched her phone. "Mentioned that you have an appointment in the morning."

"8:00."

"I'm assuming you can't drive?"

A bitter chuckle escaped me. "Not yet."

She shuffled, unwinding from the tight ball. "I'll take you. I don't work until the afternoon. It wouldn't be that big of a deal for me."

I hesitated. It didn't feel right to ask one more thing, but I couldn't deny how much it would help. Despite sleeping for twelve hours, I already felt tired again. That's what too many stupid decisions did for a man in his prime.

Made him an old man.

A growling tiger cub.

"Sure," I said. "That would be great."

A few minutes later, the sound of her settling back into the couch followed. I sat at the kitchen table, relishing the cool air conditioning as it blew on the back of my neck, and wondered.

Sometime around four, Katelyn dropped back into sleep.

* * *

"It's improving, Vik."

Those three words sent a flurry of relief all the way through my chest. For a moment, I hung my head.

"Thanks, doc."

Doc Blaine sent me a firm look. "You were lucky. We avoided compartment syndrome and a major infection. No funny business, all right? Or you'll be admitted and this agony will prolong."

I saluted.

He scoffed. "Like you've ever listened to the advice of any professional."

"Hey."

He eyed me.

I held up my hands, defenseless. "Fine, I don't have the best history, but this time I'm serious. I'm taking it easy. Don't have any job to rush back to, and I'm fine for a few more months."

Seeming relieved, he nodded. "Then you're good to go. Stay on the antibiotics, check up in ten days. I want to see the incisions. The stitches on the inside will dissolve within two weeks, but we'll remove these on the outside."

With that, he left.

The door rattled slightly after closing behind him. With a few awkward attempts, I navigated the crutches to the door and steeled myself.

In the reception area, beautiful Katelyn waited for me. She used to look nervous at the best of times, had wide eyes she tended to hide behind unnecessary designer glasses, and held a quiet curiosity about the world that she rarely satisfied. I used to know almost everything about Katelyn. She preferred poultry over red meat, was a closet chess-lover thanks to my father, and could not adore my sister more.

The Katelyn out there?

Practically an utter stranger. A stranger who knew what groceries I would want to buy, my favorite fruit, and how to give me space to be grumpy. This Kate was more confident and poised than the one I had known growing up. The Katelyn of my high school days would never have stomached the sight of a nasty wound, nor my snappy attitude yesterday.

This Katelyn had a spine.

And long hair I wanted to play with.

Her subtle-but-there expression dared me to come closer, because she was ready to push me away.

Damn, if I didn't love a challenge.

Those thoughts swirled around as I slipped out of the office, waved to a nurse that sent me a fluttering smile—never would *that* happen—and headed back to the front. The receptionist waved me away, said they'd bill my insurance, and I stood in the main area again.

Katelyn sat on one of the stuffed chairs in the lobby, head tilted back. A trivia game played across one of the screens. When one of the players missed the answer to the question *what does the letter N stand for in chess?*

"Knight, you idiot," she muttered.

I laughed.

Katelyn startled, caught my gaze, and relaxed. She was jumpier than a baby doe. The startled expression on her face fled and she quirked one of her lips up.

"Sorry, I just—"

"I get it." I held up a hand. "Everyone should know that answer."

She lifted both hands in a sign of praise, perfectly mimicking my father. "Preach it, friend." Her amusement dropped. She stood up. "Everything okay?"

I nodded. "I'm good to go home, thanks."

The ride home was as quiet as the rest of the night, the morning, and the ride over had been. As if Katelyn had a word limit and had used it up in the 3-4 sentences we'd swapped yesterday. This side of her felt strange. Chattering squirrels held nothing on Vini and Kate growing up.

Then again, Vini wasn't here.

When Kate pulled into the parking lot outside my house, her hand lingered on her gear shift.

"Need help getting in?"

"No, thanks. I have a little pride left." I smiled in case she took offense. "I can open my door."

To my relief, she returned it. "I'll come by, check on you later?"

"I'm good, thank you for all you've done. Doc Blaine says we're out of the worst. These antibiotics are working, so I just need to rest."

Katelyn smiled, but it didn't seem quite as bright. "Great, well, I left my number on the fridge in case you need anything. I work lots of random hours so . . ."

The offer, unstated, trailed into the ether. I let it go and carefully stepped out of her little four-door car. Did I want to go back into that wretched townhouse by myself? No. Being out of the drug-induced funk, and two months sober of alcohol, meant I'd get bored soon.

Boredom meant . . . not pleasant things for my state of mind.

Not being able to drive also put a big damper on dealing with my life. Suddenly, it all felt too overwhelming. I kicked those thoughts aside to tackle on my own.

I wasn't Katelyn's problem.

"Thanks again, Kate."

I shut the door and headed back to my life, leaving Katelyn firmly in the past where she'd stay, if she knew what was good for her.

Because I didn't.

KATELYN

"Earth to Katelyn?"

The sound of fingers snapping in front of my face rippled through my thoughts. I jerked back to life with a gasp.

My boss, Leslie, stood a few steps away. She peered at me, concern in her warm eyes.

"You all right?"

"Yes, sorry. Just thinking."

"He must be pretty handsome to keep your thoughts so occupied."

"No, he's—" I immediately stopped myself. Leslie illuminated like a Christmas tree and I bit back a swear word. Wow. I'd fallen *right* into that trap. Fortunately, she had mercy on me.

"I won't press for details, but you've had your head in the clouds for a week now. Hope he's worth it. In the meantime, I'm ducking across the street. We're almost out of milk and I think the ice machine is trying to break. I'll be back soon with reinforcements to get you through the rest of your shift, just in case."

She disappeared out the front door before I could thank her.

With a sigh, I gritted my teeth and let the full weight of my frustration sink in.

Oh, yes.

I'd been a space case for the last week. Only my head wasn't floating in the clouds. Instead, my heart flopped around on the ground, and I constantly searched for it. My phone buzzed in my pocket, and I hated myself for hoping—again—that Vikram had actually texted me.

No such luck.

Vinita: Hey girl! Sounds like Vik is doing much better. He's starting unsupported walking in PT, but still has another week or two before he can do it more frequently. Just wanted to thank you again for checking on him last week. How are you doing?

Katelyn: I'm glad! I hadn't heard from him so I wondered.

I stared at the message, decided it was innocuous enough, and sent it. Moments later, I regretted it and didn't know why. With a growl, I shoved my phone back in my pocket. One more reason men were trouble.

Drama, drama, drama.

Except . . . that wasn't true.

Vikram's townhouse was the first time I'd broken rules 1, 2, and 4 in over five years. Never alone, never in the dark, don't go anywhere new alone. Not only that, but I hadn't once felt afraid while there. Alone in a strange house with a man I didn't, for all intents and purposes, know that well.

Progress, certainly, but I couldn't tell Vinita.

Because there was a moment of time in his apartment—okay, several of them—when my heart raced like a mad thing. When he looked at me in surprise, I melted like butter on a hot day. The way his jaw tightened and face muscles ticked. The grace of his bare chest. While he recovered from a serious infection after surgery, I ogled him.

Really, who could blame me?

No one.

Vikram had always been poetic. His love for cooking. His obsession with recycling. His affiliation for yoga and stretching. He presented himself to the world in a I-don't-care-what-you-think kind of way, but held compassion tight in his grip.

The Vikram who spoke quietly with me in the dark had been the one I'd always secretly loved. The one I'd wanted glimpses of as often as I could find them. I saw more of the old Vik that night than the last several years combined.

Now, I just wanted to go back.

A foolish idea. I hadn't gotten his number and he hadn't used mine. Besides, Vik was a notorious womanizer. He swapped girls like I traded glasses, mostly to coordinate my outfit. Non-commitment was his thing and always had been.

Not me.

If the right guy meandered into my life and made the rules a moot point, then I'd settle into a happily ever after. Such an event seemed more and more unlikely as the years passed, because every month that ticked by made me cling to safety even more. The nightmare that I'd survived would never happen again.

Never again.

My favorite mantra.

My phone buzzed in my hand, pulling me from my spiral of darkening thoughts. Vinita popped up again, probably because I hadn't responded and I'd been standing in the middle of the coffee shop like a weirdo for five minutes.

Vinita: I need an update on your life! ASAP!

I snorted.

Katelyn: It's sad that you rely on me for excitement.

Vinita: Nah, you're epic. Any good news? Juicy gossip? Hot guys?

My teeth sank into my bottom lip. Somehow, the words *I have an eternal crush on your brother that was resurrected a week ago* just didn't roll off my fingertips so easily. No, I'd never revealed my secret. Not to Vinita or anyone.

Time to put her on a different track altogether.

Katelyn: I found some articles on birthing I think you'll like.

Vinita: Oooh? Do tell?

Relieved to throw her off the scent, I dropped a few links that I'd saved. Notes on her thoughts followed minutes later as she scanned them. I returned to her messages in between customers, my thoughts still wound around Vikram.

The phone trembled in my hand, announcing a new call, ten minutes later. I glanced at the unknown number with a frown.

Department of Corrections?

My blood turned to ice. Quickly as I could manage with an already shaking hand, I answered it and pressed the phone to my ear.

"Hello?"

The warm voice of a woman answered. "Hey there. Is this Katelyn Saucony?"

"Yes, this is Katelyn."

"Katelyn, my name is Shanice with the Department of Corrections Victim Services department. Do you have a second?"

My stomach turned into a rock. I pressed a hand to it and leaned against the counter with a breathless, "Sure."

"I'm calling to let you know that Timothy Hanover is being released in two weeks. Not this Friday, but the next Friday at noon from the Department of Corrections. The address he'll be staying at is . . . his parent's old house, I believe. 4583 Duckling road. You were signed up for a release alert, correct?"

The name echoed in my ears.

Timothy Hanover.

Timothy Hanover.

"Okay," I whispered.

So many other things surfaced that I wanted to ask instead. *Why is he getting out? What happened to his sentence? How will I stay safe? What if he makes good on his threat to kill me if I ever told anyone what happened?*

My tongue bound itself together and didn't utter a single word. Shanice's voice quieted. "Are you there, Miss Saucony?"

"Yes, I'm . . . I'm just surprised."

"If you'd like to speak with his attorney about the details, I can connect you via phone or—"

"No!" I blurted out, then instantly felt bad. "I'm sorry, no. I don't want to speak with his lawyer. I'll . . . I'll speak with mine, thank you. I appreciate the call."

"You're welcome. Please let me know if you have any other—"

I ended the call. My hands shook so hard that the phone wobbled until I set it down, afraid I'd drop it. I doubled over, pressed my forehead to the counter, and let out a long breath. I had to call Vini.

No, I couldn't call Vini.

For heaven's sake, she was pregnant and occupied trying to figure out how to give *birth*. I couldn't burden her with another stressor. If she knew that Tim was out she'd . . .

Well, what could she do?

Precisely why I couldn't tell her. Her inability to protect me would only stress her out, then affect the baby, and I wouldn't do that. I loved him too much already. Several minutes passed while I wrestled my breathing back under control.

Timothy wasn't out yet.

He was going to live at his parents old place, which put him firmly in Jackson City, a forty-five minute drive from here. He knew nothing of what was going on in my life. Or so I presumed, for we had no common acquaintances.

Truth didn't stop the shudder of terror that ripped through my body like lightning every time I thought of him. Felt the gravel scratching my back. The rain in my eyes, obscuring the hiss of his voice in my ear.

Tell anyone and I'll kill you.

Your word against mine, princess.

"Kate?"

The sound of my name jerked me out of the spiral of memories like a slap of cold water. I gasped, lifted my head, and stared right into Vikram's dark gaze. Twice I blinked, shocked to see him standing there.

Vikram.

Here.

But why?

His brow furrowed into concerned grooves, marring the high cheek bone perfection of his face. He held onto his crutches, a few steps from the counter. Hernandez stood next to him in a pair of work pants and heavy-duty boots.

"Are you all right?" Vik asked quietly.

I whirled around. I couldn't breathe. My chest tightened, throat narrowed. Holy coconuts, I was absolutely *losing* it. Tears clouded my eyes. I swallowed them back. No, I couldn't do this here.

Not here, not now.

"Fine." I swallowed back the panic, tried to slow my breaths. "I'm fine. I just . . ."

My hands shook so hard I couldn't even clasp them. The terror of hearing Timothy's name sent me right into a panic. Everything felt tight. Too tight.

So tight.

I gasped, head spinning. In moments, my knees would buckle. The world would cloud over. I knew this process well. In the right frame of mind, I'd sit on the floor so I didn't have too far to fall. My mind couldn't process how to do that right now.

A warm hand touched my shoulder.

"Hey," Vik said quietly. "It's okay."

His firm grip on my shoulder shocked me into a gasp. Breath flooded my lungs. He held on, hand heavy, like his father. A sob peeped free as he curled my back into his chest with his free arm. His left hip leaned against the counter.

"In," Vik whispered.

Like an old pattern, I fell into the command. My chest ached as I sucked in a sharp breath.

"Hold," he murmured.

The air expanded in my lungs, pressured as I obeyed.

"Out."

It whooshed out of me, through pursed lips. Vikram gave me a little squeeze, an encouragement to stay with him.

"In," he said, firmly.

Tears collected again. How had he remembered? This was the exact same routine Amma had taken me through countless times, through all kinds of circumstances. When I fled Aunt Trina's house, her skeevy boyfriends, the police raids, the parties. When I felt so afraid I couldn't breathe and stumbled into their kitchen, gasping. Amma would pull me into her, hook an arm around my chest, and breathe me through it. The rise and fall of her chest against my back had centered me.

"Hold," he murmured.

I obeyed, already calmer. The whirling sensation lost steam. My frenzy calmed. I clung to his arm, which held me so tight.

"Out."

Three cycles later, I relaxed. His hand fell away, taking warmth and anchoring with it. I closed my eyes, pulled in one last breath, and forced myself to face him. Tears lingered on my eyelashes when I met his gaze.

"Thank you."

He studied me in solemn intensity. The playful Vik I'd watched all my life had faded somewhere into the planes of this grown-up version. Life had jaded him, just like me. I wasn't sure which I understood better.

"You ready to talk about it?" he asked.

"No. Bad day, that's all. I'm fine, thank you." I forced a chipper tone that sounded more strangled than happy. I couldn't meet his gaze when I nodded to Hernandez. "Just, ah . . . weird day."

"Oh?"

"I got a call." I waved my hand to the phone. "Nothing. I just . . . everything is fine pleasedontsayawordtoVini."

The words rushed out of me in a mad stream, furthering his suspicion. Hernandez cocked an eyebrow. The panic threatened to return, but this time I had control of it and wrestled it back.

"Please?" I swallowed, a shaking hand held out. "I just had a bad day."

"Vini would understand."

"She'll read into it and she needs to focus on the baby."

"Believe it or not," Vik said wryly, "I don't rush to tell my sister everything."

Relief tripled through me.

"Thank you. I . . . thank you."

With one last, long look, he grabbed the other crutch and hobbled back around the counter. Quickly, I took their orders, grateful to hide behind the espresso machine while I gathered their drinks—and my pride—together.

Worse than embarrassing myself in front of Vikram was the fact that Timothy would soon be out of jail.

And I had no idea what that meant.

VIKRAM

Hernandez followed me out of the coffee shop, the sound of his heavy boots a firm thud on the ground. Getting out of my apartment, even coming to Pineville, had been a lifesaver.

The last-minute detour to *grab a coffee* before Hernandez took me back had a lot more to do with seeing Katelyn again.

Didn't know why, though.

Seeing her hyperventilating and in tears certainly hadn't been what I expected. Now that I'd seen it, I couldn't unsee it. Nor could I get rid of the ache in my chest that told me something wasn't right.

The door jingled as it shut behind us. I advanced a few steps into the parking lot. Hernandez followed.

"That was weird, right?" I asked.

His brow furrowed. "Yeah, really weird."

Gratified, I headed toward his truck. He unlocked the door with the fob. Balancing on one leg, I ditched the crutches in the back, hopped to the front, and climbed carefully inside. With a head full of thoughts, I grabbed the seatbelt and buckled it, then stared at the Frolicking Moose.

"She seemed scared, right?"

"Startled." Hernandez shrugged, then his gaze tapered. "Why?"

"No reason."

"Spit it, Vik."

"No reason!" I cried. "Just . . . weird."

"You wanna know what's weird? The mystic breathing crap you just pulled. You, like, sensei-ed her out of the panic attack. How'd you do it, man? Your sublime yoga powers, or something?"

I rolled my eyes. Hernandez took any opportunity to crack at my love of yoga and I wanted to punch the knowing grin off his face now.

"Katelyn is best friends with Vini."

"I remember."

"Kate used to do that all the time." I frowned as he reversed out of the spot, then spun the wheel to head toward the road. "At our house. She'd come over in a panic, unable to breathe. Amma would talk her down just like that. Seemed like what was happening now, so I put a stop to it."

Hernandez snorted. "With an aunt like hers, you'd hyperventilate too."

"Yeah?"

"Let's just say that Trina has a history."

Hernandez remained vague, but his insinuation that Katelyn's family had run-ins with law enforcement didn't shock me. He didn't bring work into his daily life, so he wouldn't give details.

Not that I needed them.

Katelyn's childhood had been anything *but* stable, that much I remembered. Details eluded me. She was my kid-sister's best friend, so I gave her about as much attention as a fly. Now, I couldn't *stop* thinking about Kate.

It took all my control not to return to the Frolicking Moose as we sped away. No reason to give Hernandez another reason to be suspicious over my motives when I didn't even understand them myself.

Whatever just happened, I didn't like the fear in her eyes. The panic. The sense of something absent, like a puzzle piece I couldn't find.

"Heard you're off the alcohol," he said.

I sent him a sidelong glance. "From who?"

"Reesa, at the liquor store."

"She has a big mouth."

"Said you haven't been there in awhile." Hernandez shot me a high-browed look. I laughed.

"Small towns are the worst."

He flashed a quick smile. "Being a deputy gets me so much information, amigo. Is it true?"

"Not your business, either way."

"Prickly," he muttered.

"Yes. It's true."

"Good." He nodded once. "Keep it that way."

I saluted with a hand. This was one road that didn't require exploring.

"Thanks," I said when the silence became burdensome. "It was nice to get out of my place for a bit. And, you know. Food."

Katelyn had stocked my place up, but with better health came a bigger appetite, and I'd zipped through the food in a few days. With my knee still on the mend, Hernandez yanked me from my hobbit-hole townhouse and forced me around people again for a few hours.

Tiring, but good.

He shrugged it off. "No problem. Next week, you're helping me at *abuela's.* She has me digging out the garden."

I laughed, but he didn't.

* * *

"C'mon, Vini," I muttered under my breath. "Pick up the da—"

Her snippy tone cut through my ear immediately.

"What?"

I reared back. "Hold off, Kingslayer. Do I need to call back?"

Vini sighed. "Sorry. Shouldn't have snapped at you. I was just falling asleep after a rough night."

"Oh. Sorry."

"No, don't be. Talk to me."

The sound of shuffling fabric made me think she'd just sat up. Guilt plagued me again. Maybe I shouldn't have ignored the fact that she didn't respond to my text messages within seconds. Regret faded quickly. I *had* to have answers.

Seven days was too long to wait. I should have texted Vini right after Kate's anxiety attack and demanded answers. I hadn't, though, because I'd promised. Now a week had passed and questions about Katelyn continued to plague me in a miserable onslaught. Beyond the annoying fact that I couldn't stop thinking about her lay a truth I also didn't want to acknowledge. I worried about her.

"How are you?" she asked. "How's the knee? Amma said you finally called her."

"I did."

"Thank you. She's been off my case for two seconds."

"Sure. Sorry again. I saw Katelyn at the Frolicking Moose a week ago and I wanted to talk to you about it."

A square of paper sat in my hand. Katelyn's number. She'd put it behind a magnet on my fridge in case I needed it. I'd long since memorized the loopy, curving numbers. Already saved it in my phone, but couldn't bring myself to use it.

"Hardly surprising," Vini murmured through a yawn. "She works there."

"Right but . . . something didn't seem right."

Vini's voice perked up. "Oh? What do you mean?"

Seconds after I explained the panic attack, the tears in her eyes, the desperate way she scrabbled herself back together, and then asked me not to tell Vini about it, the call ended. Blinking, I stared at the dark screen of my phone.

"Vini?"

Attempts to call her back were fruitless. The most logical scenario would likely mean we'd been disconnected, but I had a feeling that wasn't it. No, Vini had hung up on me. If I called Katelyn right now, it would go to voicemail.

I chewed on my bottom lip, then sat on my couch and leaned back. Nothing to do but let this play out. Whatever haunted Katelyn at work the other day now had Vini on its trail. I tilted my head back and settled in to wait.

* * *

Three minutes later, my phone buzzed. Vinita's name flashed across the screen as I answered.

"So?"

"Get to her place now." Pregnancy made her breathless all the time, but now she was doubly so. I straightened, alarmed by the panic in her voice.

"What's wrong?"

"Can you drive?"

"Yes," I drawled, glancing at my knee. "I've been driving myself to physical therapy three times a week for the last week."

"Listen, Vik, I can't tell you what's going on but I have a bad feeling. There's a guy that . . . the story isn't mine to tell, okay? Please go over there. Get your eyeballs on her. She's not answering my calls and I need to know she's okay. Then," she said in a firm tone that reminded me of Amma, "you tell her to get on that phone and call me, because if it's what I suspect, there's going to be no forgiveness for hiding it from me!"

Her voice had climbed to a shrill note. I already had my car keys in hand and one crutch under my arm. The fact that this could be a terrible idea occurred to me, but I pushed that thought away and kept going.

No.

It had been awhile since I'd done anything big for someone else. I'd been a quiet, selfish bastard for well over a year now. Maybe, on some level, I needed to do this as much as Katelyn might need me.

"I'm on it, Vini. I'll call you after I arrive."

Chapter Seven

KATELYN

"Evicted?"

The word fell off my lips in an astonished voice. I blinked, stared at the paper, then back to Teddy, my landlord. He shifted uncomfortably, porch boards creaking. He wore a wind jacket and a cowboy hat pulled low over his white hair and bulbous nose. A nose I very much wanted to punch right now.

"Sorry, kiddo." He sucked on his front teeth. "Got a grandkid that needs a place to stay. They'll be here in a week."

"You're kidding."

He shrugged. "That's the way of it."

"There are laws against this! You have to give me a reasonable notice. Two weeks, at the very least. I can't find anywhere in *Pineville* in a week."

His gaze hardened into flint and it took all my willpower not to step back. "Show me where in our contract," he muttered, "that it states such a thing."

My breath caught.

He had me there.

Desperate situations drove people to stupider things than a hastily sketched agreement to pay him cheap rent every month.

Teddy certainly had stepped in when I needed the help last winter and allowed me to rent out an apartment above his garage that he and his charming wife rarely used.

They lived in the attached house, the entrance to my apartment was in a well-lit backyard near a Jacuzzi they never used, and I didn't fear for my life in this quiet neighborhood, far off the beaten path. No apartments admitting people in and out that I didn't know. No neighbors to be concerned over.

No dark, poorly lit parking lots.

The rules were so easy to abide by here.

I closed my eyes and pulled in a deep breath. Until this moment, Teddy and I had a great rapport. I paid on the first of every month, and his wife, Betty, brought me Sunday dinners. The thought of losing that stability left a knot in my throat. I swallowed it back.

"Okay." I licked my lips. "I'll . . . figure something out."

His expression melted a little. His wife was a sweetheart, but he'd always been rough around the edges. No doubt he came to deliver the news because she wouldn't have been able to kick me out.

"I'm sorry, Katelyn. They really need the place and we can't tell them no."

I nodded. In fact, I understood. Felt a pang of jealousy for their loved-grandchild that had built-in support systems. But I didn't have the words to say it, just nodded and closed the door.

The paper trembled when I pressed my back to the door and slid down. A calendar near the door, sprinkled with cartoons that always made me laugh, caught my eyes. Vini had given it to me at Christmas. *So you think of me every day and laugh,* she'd said.

A week ago, I'd drawn a fat black square around the day when Tim would be released. It loomed there, an ugly scar on white paper.

One week away.

Fan-freaking-tastic.

My heart nearly jumped out of my chest when a knock came on my door, followed by a tentative, "Katelyn?"

I sucked in a sharp breath.

Vikram?

I scrambled to my feet, shoved my hair out of my eyes, and jammed my glasses back on. I didn't need them to see, I just loved to have them there. A barrier. Something to hide behind or have an excuse to get away from awkward situations. Like a superpower you used only when needed. I fumbled with the door knob as I pulled it open an inch and peered out.

My heart leapt in my throat.

Holy coconuts, it *was* Vikram.

The moment he saw me, his gaze tapered. "You all right?" he asked. I nodded, not trusting myself to speak. His hair hung behind his back in a neat ponytail, out of the way. A hint of stubble graced his cheeks. I wanted to reach back, loosen the ponytail, and run my fingers through it.

Silk, I imagined.

"Hey," I managed.

"Hey." He frowned. "You don't look so good."

"Fine." My attempt at a cheerful voice fell like a bomb. Why did this keep happening? Did he have radar for the worst moments of my life? "I'm good, thanks."

His gaze darted around, then back to me.

"Can I come in?"

I hesitated. No, of course he couldn't. The rules. They were there . . . no. They didn't really apply to him, did they? The one man I felt safe with. That I would beg to stand closer simply because everything felt not so frightening with him at my side.

Hadn't Vikram always been a rule bender? A rule breaker?

Yes. Always. Somehow, he'd also done it for me and my iron-clad rules. With a reluctant nod, I opened the door. He didn't take his studious gaze off of me as he stepped inside, crutches under his arm.

"Can you do stairs?"

He nodded. Silently, we ascended the stairs that led to my studio, which was even smaller than the loft above the Frolicking Moose. Definitely older. Shabby it might be, but that meant nothing against safety.

My mind raced in the short time that I had to figure out why he'd come. How did he know where I lived? Why was he here?

What was happening with the world's juju these days?

As we stepped up the creaky old stairs—another perk because no one ever snuck up on me—the puzzle pieces came together. The only way Vikram could have known where to find me was his sister. No one at the Coffee Shop would give him my address, and I doubted Hernandez knew.

A flash of rage followed.

He must have called Vinita. Practically trembling with it, I pushed through the door at the top of the stairs. Light flooded the staircase behind me. I grabbed a jacket hanging off the back of a chair and wrapped it around me, stuffing my hands in the pockets.

When I spun around, Vik stood in the doorway. Instead of checking out the old room, he watched me.

Warily.

He *should* be on guard.

My jaw felt tight when I stopped and faced him fully. He closed the door behind him, eyes finally roving.

"Vinita," I said, and couldn't help the way it sounded like an accusation. "She's worried. You told her that I had a panic attack so she sent you over here with my address to check on me."

He opened his mouth, then closed it again.

"Uh, yeah."

His gaze dropped and he cleared his throat. He could swim in that guilt until his toes looked like prunes for all I cared.

He called Vinita!

I ran a hand over my face, grateful for the surge of annoyance. Like a rising tide, it carried me past the trepidation over Timothy and needing to find a new place and . . .

"Okay," I finally said when I couldn't take the unapologetic quiet any further. His eternally brown eyes had a touch of guilt to them. "So we're going to have to deal with Vinita first. I'm assuming she's waiting for me to call back."

I began to pace, shaking my head as I mentally sifted through my options. Words were important here. Vinita read into every tone and nuance. Now that she was pregnant and not working in the office as much, she had the time to dissect each stinking syllable—and she would.

"That's not first," Vikram countered. "First: are you okay?"

His voice rolled all the way through me with a shiver. I turned away.

No.

Definitely not okay.

But not *not* okay, even though that didn't make sense.

I forced myself to meet his gaze.

"Just a run of a few bad days. I'll figure it out. It'll . . . it'll pass. And *yes*," I snapped, "that is the first step. My house, my rules."

Except it wasn't my house. Not anymore.

"What are you figuring out?"

I acted like I hadn't heard the question as I grabbed my phone out of my back pocket. A new text message waited from Kinoshi, my local attorney. My stomach clenched. What impeccable timing. I ignored it for later.

No doubt it was a response to my panicked email about placing a restraining order against Timothy, and Kinoshi's opinion on whether I had time to legally change my name. Hair color was easy enough, though I loved being blonde . . .

I'd do it in a heartbeat.

Anything for safety.

"Kate," he drawled. "Are you okay?"

I realized too late that I'd fallen into thought. I shook myself out of it.

Vikram cocked an eyebrow to punctuate the question, then tilted his head. His deeper perusal made my shoulders clench. I knew what that ticking jaw meant. The brewing trouble in his gaze, hidden behind what looked like amusement, but was actually calculation.

For a moment, I wondered if I *could* tell Vikram the whole, hideous truth, but dismissed the thought as quickly as it came.

No.

Fortunately, I had a new problem.

"My landlord just delivered some unexpected news. I have seven days to get my stuff and find a new place. He only gave me a week's notice."

A frustrated raspberry escaped me. Vinita had texted me thirteen times. Thirteen. Her record was thirty-four, but that happened a few months after the assault when my phone had accidentally been turned off. I hadn't seen them, so I didn't respond. She panicked for hours.

The very last text sent a shot of weariness through me.

Vinita: Is it Tim? It's Tim isn't it. They called you to notify you.

With a ragged sigh, I wrote back.

Katelyn: He will be released next week.

A stream of curse words followed without spaces.

Vikram frowned, oblivious to our text message discussion.

"That sucks you were evicted, and we'll get back to that in just a moment, but there must be something else. Your panic attack was last week. Sounds like your landlord just dropped that bomb tonight. So what's up? What are you hiding?"

Too late, I realized my mistake. Vikram's tenacity was legendary. Fortunately, I wasn't the wilting flower he grew up with anymore.

Still . . . did he have to comprehend things so quickly?

His question was a bold one considering we barely knew each other—at least as adults. I'd waltzed into his life a few weeks ago, and now he barged into mine like a beautiful, avenging god.

"I'm going to call Vinita." I held up my phone. "First priority, always."

He reached over, plucked the phone from my hand, and set it on the counter next to me. I could still reach it, but knowing he had the audacity to take it from me forced me to pause. My mouth dropped open.

He lay the full power of those dark eyes on me.

"Kate, do you need help?"

Grit carried me through years of mostly-unstable living with my mother, then my aunt. Aunt Trina's rotating boyfriends, each more troublesome and drug-addled than the rest, wreaked havoc on my life and safety. Grit salvaged me back together when Trina kicked me out of the house at sixteen. Grit rushed me into the arms of Vinita's family around the street, where I worked to pay for my own car, my own gas, but still lived on their hospitality and love.

The same grit escorted me through the worst experience of my life five years ago. It had never failed me, not once.

Said grit absolutely crumbled now.

With Vikram right in front of me, dreams from my youth weakened my resolve. On the scariest nights at Trina's, with music thumping and druggies looking for a room to take another hit, and Trina's screeching laughter above all of it, I'd hide in my closet, screw my eyes shut, and think of Vikram.

His arms around me.

His fingers patting down my hair, telling me everything was fine. I was safe, loved, and not alone. The daydreams distracted me then, little more than vague shadows. Tendrils of promises. Now, they served as a reminder to just how little Vik and I knew each other, despite spending much of my life near him.

The power of that history was the only thing that gave me the courage to whisper, "Yes. I need help."

His expression relaxed.

"Good," he murmured. "Because I'm here to give it."

* * *

We sat at my table over cups of tea.

He chose a mellow chamomile.

I chose spicy, bold chai.

They both felt like a lie.

My fingers fidgeted with the tea bag, plunking it up and down, as I explained what Teddy said. Vikram leaned back in his chair, leg propped on another chair, with casual ease. A tendril of hair escaped his ponytail, near his temple. I watched it instead of his eyes to keep my courage.

"Not sure how much you know about the housing market here," I murmured, "but there aren't a lot of safe options for me to rent."

He made a sound like a grunt, accompanied by a nod. I had a sip of the now-lukewarm tea—his was almost gone—and didn't even taste the cinnamon as it rushed over my tongue.

When he said nothing, I babbled to fill the silence.

"I'm not sure if the Frolicking Moose is rented out, so I think I'll try there first. It'll buy me some time. Maybe."

To my relief, he nodded, as if he approved. Having someone

else's stamp of okayness felt better than wading into the void on my own. The Frolicking Moose loft doubled as a HomeBnb, and tended to book out quickly. Patches of availability appeared here and there.

I hoped.

His phone buzzed, but he ignored it.

"It's Vini," I said.

He sighed. "I know. I'm avoiding her." He met my gaze over the top of his phone. "I'm sorry, Kate. I wasn't trying to get you in trouble. I've just been worried, that's all. I can't get you out of my head," he mumbled.

His sincerity—despite a slightly annoyed tone—cut all the way through my heart. Such an apology was a gallant move that re-stole my loyalty all over again.

"Oh." I pressed my lips together and shook my head. "It's fine. I shouldn't have reacted that way. I'm sorry."

He waved it off, then answered the phone with a quick, "Vini."

Her voice jabbered, words indistinguishable, though I could detect nuances of frustration in the speed. Vik sent me an amused glance, then turned his attention back to the phone.

"I'm at her place. Yeah. She's being evicted."

My eyes closed. Frankly, I had no energy to be frustrated again. Instead, I accepted his help with gratitude. Vik had just removed the burden of dealing with Vini's loving outrage off my shoulders. I opened one eye to find him good-naturedly rolling his eyes as he pointed to the phone.

Eventually, Vini's tirade slowed.

"No, Vini, she's not going to be homeless and she's not moving to New York to live with you and Zayne."

He looked at me, one eyebrow cocked in question.

I shook my head. Definitely not going to New York. Living with Vini was a dream of mine, but would make for a terrible marriage. Zayne would never see his wife, and I'd intrude on their happily-ever-after. We needed independence.

"Vini, calm down. Everything is all worked out."

Vik met my gaze, holding it. My soul crinkled all the way to my toes under the power of that stare.

I pulled in a breath as he murmured, "She's going to stay with me."

Chapter Eight

VIKRAM

The moment the words dropped from my lips, the unsettled feeling in my chest finally calmed. A week of restless agony—gone in a breath.

Katelyn's astonished expression morphed into confusion, then something not unlike terror. Vini's incessant chattering in my ear went silent.

"What?"

I leaned forward, speaking more for her sake now than Vini, but wanted to buy Katelyn a few moments. "Katelyn is going to stay with me. Hernandez and I will help her pack. You remember my place, right? There's plenty of room in the hall closet for storage and she'll have the whole back bedroom."

Vini fell silent.

"Well," she murmured. "That's not half bad, you know."

Kate's brow had grown heavy over her lovely eyes. She kept her gaze locked on the table, but didn't seem trepidatious. Thoughts swirled behind those turtle-shelled glasses as she pieced together variables, options, arguments. Oh, I saw her attempts to thwart this.

Eternal Second at her best.

Years apart notwithstanding, I knew *exactly* how to play this chessboard. "Is there anything safer in Pineville?" I queried. "She can move in tonight."

Katelyn's head popped up.

Bingo.

Any crumbling uncertainty disappeared in a slow landslide. She blinked rapidly, then closed her eyes and sighed.

Resignation.

Ah, victory.

Vinita let out a long breath. "Vik," she said, "Are you sure?"

"Yes."

"There's . . . look, there's more going on here than it appears. Kate . . . it's, again, not my story to tell. But suffice to say that she needs you. All right? Don't let her talk you out of it. She needs a big brother more than ever."

The hell with that, I almost said, but stopped myself. There would be nothing big-brotherly about my relationship with Katelyn.

Protective, yes.

Big brother? No.

"Got it," I said. "We'll call you later."

Before Vini could boss me around and tell me how to pack, I closed the call and set my phone on the table. Katelyn regarded me like she wasn't sure whether I'd explode or say something else sort-of stupid.

"If you have something else that's better," I said quietly, "then let me know, but it sounds like your best option."

Katelyn swallowed and lifted her chin. Pride—or something like it—drove her gaze into mine.

"Thank you for the offer, Vik. I appreciate your gallant offer, but I don't accept it." She swallowed hard. "Yet. I'll let you know in a week after I've looked at my options."

And that was that.

* * *

The week passed in inhumane ways—and not just because I didn't receive one call, email, or text message from Katelyn. Meanwhile, physical therapy drove into beast mode.

Shucking off the crutches—the embarrassment of how much sweat I broke with their simple exercises—took a grueling center stage. Thinking of all the alpine climbs, hikes, and yoga poses I used to execute so easily didn't help. Dangling over a watery precipice in my twenties, held by only my fingers, flashed through my mind often while I labored to walk on my own without pain.

Katelyn's eyes filled my thoughts next.

When a weird silence caught my ear, I glanced up. Bastian stared at me from across the table, a burrito in his hand. He lifted an eyebrow in silent question, because Bastian only used words when he absolutely had to.

I shook my head.

"Sorry, what did you say?"

"Hernandez said you have a girl now." Bastian paused a breath away from taking a bite. He didn't finish his question, but the rest lingered in his eyes.

"Hernandez is an idiot."

My sore knee left me in a crabby mood, not to mention the blank screen on my phone. Lunch with Bastian didn't help. Why it got under my skin so much that Katelyn hadn't responded, I'd never understand.

Bastian tore into his burrito. I shoved rice around my bowl with a fork, then dropped it.

"But there is something."

A shot of amusement crossed his eyes, but he had the wisdom not to let a smile show. Not while I was *this* agitated. Instead he leaned back, motioned for me to continue with a rise of his brow, and grabbed his drink for a quick pull.

"It's Katelyn. You remember her? Vinita's friend."

He paused, then nodded.

"She popped back into my life unexpectedly, helped me out, and is back out of it again. She might need help but won't let me give it, and she's skittish, like a deer. Super evasive. It's been three weeks, and I've seen her twice. Once because I sort of forced her into it."

Bastian frowned. "Wasn't she always like that?"

I shrugged. "This is different."

"Huh."

He ran his tongue over his teeth, then took another bite. I nudged guacamole into a corner of the bowl, thoughts churning.

"Vinita said there's some recent history that she won't tell me about. Don't know what it means, but Katelyn appears . . . frightened."

"Ah." Bastian's features illuminated. "You always loved being the hero."

"Shut up."

He held up two hands, laughing. "What? You were the ladies' man. Always. Women flock to you."

"Not this one."

He laughed again. "That explains it."

I scowled. "No, that doesn't. Katelyn isn't a conquest to win or a challenge or even a distraction. She's . . . different."

"Sure."

I opened my mouth to tell him *exactly* what I thought of his amusement, but our waitress approached. She looked right at me, a bright smile on her face.

"Can I get either of you anything?"

"No, I'm good."

"Nothing?"

She leaned against the table, eyes batting my direction. As far as subtlety went, she had none of it. A year ago, I would have hopped on that in a second. Dinner, date, who-knew-what-else. Too easy, girl.

Today?

I turned away.

"Nothing."

After a pause, she disappeared. Bastian smirked.

I threw a piece of chicken at him.

Bash leaned forward, exasperated. Grains of rice dribbled out of his burrito as he pushed the plate forward to make room for his arms.

"Since when are you hung up on a woman?"

"Since now."

"Huh."

"You're the one in a committed relationship. Any words of advice?"

He rolled his eyes. "Don't tell me you're still bitter about me and Dahlia being together?"

I frowned. "Dahlia's great."

"You hate that the Merry Idiots have moved into their own lives, and you haven't."

Not entirely wrong. The hard, plastic seats edged into my back. I shifted uncomfortably and held up both hands.

"There's nothing wrong with your choices. Grady is happily married. Hernandez too." My lips pulled up—saying the words felt too weird. "And you're with Dahlia for life, or whatever. Personally, I don't get it, but I'm happy that you're happy."

Bastian lifted an eyebrow. A thousand words seemed to cross his expression, then fade. He shook his head, exasperation palpable.

"Yeah," he murmured. "You're right."

My brow lifted in shock.

"I'm *right*?"

"You don't get it."

My glare brought further amusement. He shrugged with

one shoulder, then lounged back. His long body didn't quite fit in this little booth.

"You want advice? Here's my advice: Don't screw it up. Stop pouting. If you want the girl, go after the girl. Your track record is perfect."

"It won't work. Not this time."

He had the gall to appear impressed. "Sounds like you finally found a keeper."

His laugh ripped through the room as I flipped him off.

Chapter Nine

KATELYN

Leslie's nails tapped the top of the counter as she regarded her calendar, then me. Blonde hair dangled in front of her face on either side, pulled out of her eyes in a half-ponytail on top of her head. A frown marred her lovely features.

"Sorry, Kate. The loft is booked. You know how crazy summer is."

"All summer? No availability?"

She shook her head.

Right. Not that I should be surprised. My mind drifted to my apartment, where everything lay in boxes near the front door, neatly stacked. Everything I owned on this planet could be packed into my little car. For some reason, that made me unaccountably sad.

"Okay. Thanks for checking."

She lowered the calendar and tilted her head. "Something you want to talk about?"

"No," I said quickly. "Just asking for a friend."

A bright smile put her off my trail, but only because the door opened and a customer drifted inside. Leslie wandered into the office while I returned to the register, my stomach a hot mess of nerves.

If it hadn't been summer—if they'd just evicted me three months earlier or later—I might have had a prayer at finding last-minute accommodations. As it stood, I had no hope of finding a place to stay, even if money hadn't been an issue.

It definitely was an issue. I had unresolved debts with Kinoshi to pay, and potentially more upcoming now that Tim was back out of jail. The last five years had been a comedy of errors while I attempted to hold down a normal life, a job, and the costs of a desperately-needed therapist. The lack of stability led me right back home to Pineville.

I smiled at a mother-daughter pair that stepped up to the counter, then proceeded with their orders. Once they left, my gaze drifted outside. No, I couldn't keep watching the sidewalk. Couldn't expect Tim to show up at any moment, even though today was the day they released him.

Wasn't there a probation period, or something?

Did he go *right* home?

For all I knew, he was already home and enjoying dinner and a steak, or still in the jail waiting for a ride. A vague glimmer of something reminded me that his parents had both died in the last five years. Stroke, for his father. Lung cancer for his mother.

All the work that I'd been through with my therapist—a close friend and colleague of Vinita's whom she'd worked with before—surfaced through my mind in layers. While therapy had served me well over the past several years, knowing Timothy was out in the world hit me like a cold wave.

A shockwave.

I still trembled in my very center, afraid of what Timothy's release could mean. Likely, nothing. Who wanted to go back to prison, anyway? Timothy might go into his life and live away from me forever.

Or he might be *really* angry that I spoke out, pressed charges, testified against him, and stared right into his livid eyes when they took him away after the trial. For days, I'd shaken on and off as I thought about it. Even now, the memory sent a chill through me. This level of paranoia would kill me by the end of the week.

After that?

Homelessness.

Once the shop cleared again, I returned to my phone. Dahlia had two potential contacts at the RV park that might have trailers to rent. A long shot, of course, but even a temporary bandaid was welcome.

The vague thought that I tried a little *too* hard to avoid Vikram filtered through my mind, but I sent it back out again.

Two replies had already come in from the exploratory text messages I sent out.

RVPark World: We have one slot for the next week. A pull through.

I frowned.

Katelyn: Any trailers to rent?

RVPark World: Trailers? No, you have to supply those.

I chewed on my bottom lip and set the phone aside. Of course. That had been an idiotic hope. The small savings that I'd built up over the last couple of years burned in my bank account. With it as a supplement, I could afford an apartment in Jackson City for three months, and the cost of gas would eat up most of my paycheck.

Vikram floated back through my mind.

He'd given me plenty of distance since his offer, which had been a relief. I needed space to think without his beautiful head interrupting it. My phone buzzed on the counter. The flash of Vinita's name sent a dual feeling of terror and relief through me at the same time. For several moments, I debated whether to answer it.

At the last second, I picked it up with my happy-to-see-your-name voice on point.

"Hey!"

"So I've got this figured out," Vinita said. "There are some apartment places on the southern edge of Jackson—"

"Already looked yesterday. They're garbage. Super scary. Not sure how old those pictures are on the listing online, but they don't look like that anymore."

Vinita swore under her breath.

"No HomeBnb's available in the area." I ticked my fingers off one by one as I spoke, even though she couldn't see me. "No locals that have an extra room, no RV's to rent. I think I may end up camping."

She hissed.

I managed a laugh.

"Just kidding."

A pause swelled between us. "Why don't you just take Vikram's offer?" she asked quietly. "I know he meant it. You know Vik. He would never have offered if he didn't mean it. And, you *know* you'd be safe with him."

My belly burned with the truth of it. I would be safe with Vikram. Arguably, he was the only person I had felt safe with, despite not interacting with him for years. If Timothy's release didn't loom over me, this wouldn't have been nearly as stressful.

"I . . ."

I hesitated.

Did Vinita know how I felt about her brother? Highly doubtful. All my life, I'd kept the crush under wraps, leaving him to simmer in my dreams. To admit it now felt juvenile, but so did hiding it.

"I don't think it would be wise for me to stay with Vikram."

"Why not?"

Concern, more than surprise, filled her tone.

"Ah . . . let's just say that for most of our childhood, I harbored a bit of a crush on him."

Vinita burst out laughing. My cheeks flooded with heat. I ducked my head, checking out of the corner of my eye to make sure no one else approached. It would be mortally embarrassing if he happened to stroll into the shop right now.

Trust my luck for that.

"A bit of a crush?" Vini cried, giggling. "Katelyn, my darling, you were flat out hopeless and moon-eyed over him."

My jaw dropped. "You knew?"

"Who didn't?"

"Vikram," I whispered, feeling the blood drain from my face. "Please tell me Vikram didn't know."

Vinita continued to giggle. "No, I don't think he did. Truly. He saw you like a little sister, too busy with all the ladies his own age that he chased." She sobered slightly. "As he should have because you were too young for him at the time. Regardless, why would that matter now?"

My throat nearly closed off. At my silence, Vini whispered, "Oh. Do you . . . do you still feel that way?"

Hiding anything from her was hopeless. "Maybe," I wrenched out.

"Well."

When no further reply came, I groaned and put my head in my hands.

"Vini, what am I going to do? I can't find anywhere to stay. I have to be gone in the morning and everything is packed and . . . Timothy is out there now. I'll never feel safe in a new place myself. What if . . ."

"First of all," Vini said with a little snap. "You're safe. You're going to be fine. Your rules have kept you physically safe—we won't go into emotional ramifications right now, save that for later—and you'll continue to do that. You are known and loved in Pineville. For the moment, it *is* the safest place for you. Until we can move you to New York," she added lightly.

I snorted.

She joked—we always did—because I'd never move that far from Pineville. I clung to it as the only place that belonged to *me*.

"Secondly, you might have a crush on my brother. Who doesn't? He's charming and beautiful and totally messed up in the head. Every woman's dream. They all want to fix him and he loves that, then he runs away. That's not you, right? It's *so* not you," she said before I could answer. "Right now, we're prioritizing your physical safety over everything. You need a place to stay and someone to keep you safe. That's Vik."

"What if Timothy comes?"

"Then good luck, brother," she muttered. "Vik would tear his eyes out."

Even with a knee injury, I silently agreed. Vikram could take a weasel like Timothy in a heartbeat.

Where had he been five years ago?

I closed my eyes. "You're right. I'm being silly. Vikram is like my brother. He's offering me a safe spot. I'm . . . grateful. I will take it with gratitude and thanks."

Vini cheered. "Amma will be so proud! Besides," she added grandly, clearly delighted, "what if something *did* happen between you and Vik? I'd absolutely die of happiness. *Die,* I tell you."

"Vini, don't you—"

"I won't." I pictured her holding two hands in the air in her usual dramatic way. "No meddling hens here, just know I'm rooting for you. How does that plan feel?"

The thought of staying with Vik released a burden from my chest. Until now, I hadn't realized how much courage it had been pressing out of my heart. I closed my eyes and released a sigh.

"So much better."

"Exactly. I'm here to help you through it. I swear it," she said with a little trill, "my lips are sealed. Vikram will only know how much you've always loved him when you tell him the words yourself."

* * *

Twilight sparkled when I pulled up to Vikram's townhouse.

My hand trembled as I shoved the car into park. I should have texted him to confirm I could still stay. Let him know I was on my way. After turning the key in to Teddy and doing one last sweep of the little space, though, I'd run out of courage.

I just drove.

Now, I sat in my car, out of place, conspicuous, and desperate to get inside. Rule #4 sped through my mind—*don't go anywhere new alone.*

Well, this wasn't exactly a new place.

It just felt like it.

I swallowed hard.

"C'mon, Kate," I muttered. "You can do this."

With the last gust of bravery I had, I shoved the car door open. Vini always said that the most important step into a better life was the next one. To think of the step ahead or behind would only distract. I clung to her wisdom, one step at a time.

I pulled my messenger bag over my shoulder as I walked up the short flight of stairs to the front door. My car lights beeped as I locked it. No sound issued from inside when I gently rapped on the door.

My heart sat in my throat, making it hard to breathe. Feet approached, then slowed. The door knob twisted and Vik's dark eyes appeared.

His curious gaze softened into a little smile.

"Hey."

Electricity shot all the way through my body, cracking out from my toes and back into the earth. The world shifted underneath me, and I wondered how he didn't feel the aftershocks.

The door widened as he opened it with his left arm. He stood on both feet now, only one crutch under his left armpit. Everything about him swamped me with relief. Thoughts of homelessness and Timothy fled.

For the first time, I *felt* like I'd come home.

With a tilt of his head, he said, "Come on in, Kate. I've got everything ready for you."

Chapter Ten

VIKRAM

Katelyn reminded me of a cornered rabbit.

Darting.

Quick.

Suspicious. Frail, but tenacious.

Together, we unpacked her car in a few trips. I carried a clothes bag, a laundry basket, and a few other smaller things she'd stashed into the passenger seat with my right arm while I hobbled with my left crutch. The injured knee took the weight I offered it. Kate carefully lugged boxes behind her into my living room while I shoved dinner onto a back burner and grabbed a few extra bags in the back seat.

After she looked through her car and came inside, she closed the door. The *snick* of the lock closing behind her startled me, but when I looked over, she was slipping out of her shoes. Her hand fidgeted with the end of her sleeve.

"Come on. I'll show you the room in the back."

Out of instinct, I grabbed her arm to tug her toward the hallway on the right. She immediately resisted, body tightening. Without missing a beat, I let go and chattered about dinner, as if nothing awkward had happened.

Amma always told me I was too touchy by half. It was one of my greatest issues in high school. Girls misinterpreted my attention all the time, and I rarely meant it as seriously as it might have come across.

Still, Kate's response was . . . interesting.

"Your room is down here, right next to mine. We'll have to share the bathroom, if you're okay with that. You'll take the room on the right, I have the left."

My door was wedged open, spilling light into the simple, clean interior. If I'd gotten anything from Appa, his obsession with cleanliness was it. She glanced inside, then quickly away. We stepped through her doorway next. She stopped, eyes wide.

Her silence made me nervous.

"Think it'll be okay?" I asked.

Katelyn strode over, picked up the picture of my parents dancing under fireworks during Diwali. She hugged it to her.

"This is my favorite picture of them. Did you know that?"

"Lucky guess."

"This room is wonderful. I . . . thank you."

Before she could work herself into an awkward tizzy, I lifted a hand. "Ready for house rules?" I asked.

She rolled her lips together and nodded like a teenager about to get a life sentence. The picture made a gentle *thunk* as she set it back down.

"First, no thanking me."

Her expression crinkled into a frown, but I waved a hand.

"Stop. Stop. You're a . . . friend."

The word nearly choked me, because I'd almost said *family* but couldn't tolerate that word. Not as it applied to Katelyn. No way in hell would I think about the curve of her hips or the gentle slope of her neck if she was part of my family.

Firm boundary.

"I'm always happy to help out where I can," I continued, before I asked if I could kiss her. "Second, no cleaning the bathroom, because that's gross. Only I should have to clean the bathroom as owner of this townhouse. Third, help yourself to anything—food, space, TV, whatever."

"That's it?"

"You're going to have to live with me, and that is punishment enough."

The corners of her mouth twitched. She managed a wry smile. Living with her delightful mannerism?

This wouldn't suck at all.

"Right," she declared with resolve. "This is most excellent and big and will be perfect and exceeds all expectations. Can we . . ." She licked her lips. I almost lost my mind at the unintentionally sexy gesture. "Can we discuss rent while we're on the topic of rules? How much—"

"No," I said brightly. "Thank you. That is rule number four."

"Vik!"

Ignoring her, I spun. "No speaking of rent. Rule number 4. Go ahead and get settled. Dinner'll be ready in twenty."

"But—"

I held up a hand. She stopped, snorted, and then sighed.

I grinned as I exited the room, headed toward simmering spices and sambar.

Victory was mine.

* * *

Katelyn wandered into the kitchen fifteen minutes later, after she'd carried the final boxes into her new room. The clatter of toothbrushes and the hum of dresser drawers opening and closing followed. While the kitchen filled with the aromatic symphony of red chilis and coriander seeds, she filled the rest of my place with sound.

I missed noise.

Being a bachelor had been my life path, but the quiet affected me every now and then. Amma's nagging voice, telling me to *find a woman and get married, already!* tagged along with me every day.

The past month or two had been the worst of it. Having no one to help me with recovery kept me low. Not being out on the dating scene had been replenishing and . . .

Boring.

"Dosas?"

Her bright question came from the doorway between the kitchen and the living room. I grinned.

"A forever favorite."

She closed her eyes, drawing in a deep breath.

"The sambar smells perfect. Just like your Amma."

"Don't insult me. Both of them *are* perfect. Steel bowls are in the cupboard on the left if you want to grab a couple. Spoons for the sambar are below that."

The assignment pulled her into the kitchen without awkwardness. Ten minutes later, we cluttered the table with piping hot sambar and dosas cooling on a plate. She grabbed a dosa with her fingers, tearing into it without utensils—just the way we liked it.

Hunger made it easy to relax into conversation in between bites. I steered topics to anything except moving, being here, or whatever had happened the last week to land her on my porch. I was just relieved she'd shown up.

Safe.

Why my head was so focused on Katelyn, I couldn't say. Call it a hunch, but I'd long learned to listen to my instincts.

She needed me.

A text came from Vini, jarring the phone in my pocket. I ignored it. Katelyn set down her spoon, plate empty, and reached for a paper towel to wipe the grease off her hands.

"Thank you for dinner," she said. "It . . . tasted like home."

A smile accompanied her words, and I knew she thought of Amma. Advancing into my early thirties had taught me a lot of lessons, the greatest of which was gratitude toward the stability that my parents provided. Growing up, I hadn't realized how much I had. Through Katelyn's eyes, I saw it now.

"You ever go back to the old neighborhood?" I asked, gathering our plates. She stood up, plucking the used napkins off the table.

"No. You?"

"Not since my parents moved out." I hobbled to the sink, plates held in one hand, crutch in the other. "Sometimes I drive by the high school, though."

She laughed. "I've definitely not returned there. Nothing about leaving high school made me sad, except losing access to Vini." Her voice softened with nostalgia.

"You really love her," I stated, setting the plates in the sink. She bustled at my back, replacing things, opening cupboards. I let her get a lay for the land as she skimmed through drawers.

"She's my best friend."

"You're the other half of her heart, you know that?"

A wide smile split her face, one I'd like to see again.

And again.

"I do. It's the same for me."

Silence filled the kitchen as she wiped down the table, dried the dishes as I washed them. The gentle movements were easy as long as I leaned against the cupboard and kept the weight off my knee. Any normalcy was a breath of fresh air.

"I'm going to bed." Katelyn backed toward the doorway, a hand in her back pocket, teeth worrying her bottom lip. "Is there any routine that I need to know about or—"

"Nah. I shower in the mornings. I'm an early riser, around 6, but I can keep things quiet."

"I open most days, so I'll be gone before 4:00 in the morning."

"Ugly," I muttered. "I mean, I like early mornings, but that is *early.*"

She smiled. "I don't mind. It's like I have the world to myself. Anyway, thank you again for dinner and for giving me a place to crash. I'm sure I'll be able to find something else soon so I'm out of your way."

My attempt to protest fell on an empty kitchen.

Kate was already gone.

* * *

A blast of heat swept over me when I sat in my car, grimacing.

My knee smarted—in a lot of good ways—but still didn't feel ready. The healed-over incision had a nice pink tinge to it, indicating great progress. The bulky, black brace annoyed me every day, but it was better than the pain. At least I could drive myself with full physician approval.

"Astounding progress." Jake, my physical therapist had said. "Keep up the good work, Vik. You can toss those crutches aside now, unless you feel like you need them. Use them as support if you're tired. Our next goal is to get the brace off next week, then we'll focus on your ten weeks post-op goal. We're not far away. Each week, you'll be able to walk unassisted a little bit longer."

The car purred when I started it. I shoved the air vents to the side, threw on my seat belt, and backed out of the parking lot. Before I built up steam on the highway headed back to Pineville, the phone rang. I saw the name on the screen and groaned.

No avoiding it now.

A familiar voice sang through the car. "Hello Vikram, my favorite son who never calls his Amma."

"Hello Amma. *Hegidiya?*" I drawled dutifully.

"How did it go with Katelyn?" she demanded, because Amma never *asked* anything. "Is she okay? Did you get everything moved in? She's working and hasn't responded, but she's normally dealing with the breakfast rush until almost noon in the summer. Were you nice to her? Did you make her some dosas?"

"Your knowledge of her schedule is sort of creepy."

She made a rude noise. "What? We text all the time."

"I know you do."

"And she's like my daughter. I consider her my daughter!"

The words twisted something inside me. "I know that also. Everything is fine, Amma. I haven't bitten her on the full moon, we moved her stuff inside in less than twenty minutes, and she's been here five days. So far, it's been hit or miss whether we see each other. I'm gone when she's there, and she's gone when I'm there."

Unfortunately, that was true.

Kate seemed hell-bent on staying for as short a time as she must. When she didn't work, she scoured Pineville, Jackson City, and local listings for a place to live. Summertime actively worked against her. I could only hope she'd get tired of searching and give in, already. I had a dark feeling she avoided me on purpose.

Why, I couldn't fathom.

"Has she had any more panic attacks?" Amma asked.

"No."

"Good."

Aside from a few getting-locked-out incidents, everything had been smooth sailing. She had an obsession with the house being locked while she was inside—or outside, for that matter.

"I approve of your report." Amma's rattled tone smoothed out. "I'm happy to hear all of that. Now that the most important person is covered, how are you?"

I scoffed. "Most important person, huh?"

Through the phone, I could feel her grin. "You know what I mean."

Actually, it didn't bother me.

"Really, Vik. How's the knee?" she continued, "I'm still frustrated with you for not keeping us updated better, but I'm willing to let it slide." Her voice softened. "I wish I could have been there to help you."

"I know, Amma, but you're where you need to be. And everything with the knee is fine. We're five weeks post-op now, and I can get off crutches now. I get the brace off next week."

"When will you go back to work?"

"Not sure," I murmured, conveniently setting aside the fact that, after I used up six weeks of leave, my job with the trains would end.

So would my health insurance.

Had to figure that one out.

Confusion clouded Mum's voice. "You're not going back to the trains? I thought—"

"Not quite sure yet, Amma. I'm looking at something else. I have an appointment with the surgeon next week, and the physical therapist thinks he'll clear me for part-time work that doesn't require lifting."

"Oh."

Silence.

If Appa had been on the phone, he would have chided me for *not getting the tech job I lined up for you out of college. It had great benefits!*

My lack of stability had always bothered my parents, though I didn't mind it much. Computers. Anemic overhead lights. None of that appealed to me. Working with trains had been a metaphorical finger-in-the-air to rigidity and expectations as a teenager, then I stuck with it. Now, I wanted something else.

Just wasn't sure what that would be.

"What else are you considering?" Amma asked.

"Something temporary until I figure out the next step." I shrugged. "I don't know. I'm not really tied into much except our boys' trip to the rain forest in South America in the fall."

She made a raspberry sound that reminded me so much of Vini, I almost laughed.

"Travel and play. That's all you ever think about. Have you met any women lately? What about getting married and having kids? You won't find a girl once you cross thirty-five!"

My mind fluttered to Katelyn, then away.

"No."

"Are you going on dates?" she amended, and I laughed.

"Also no."

She huffed. "You're lucky your sister is giving me a grand-baby soon, or else I'd be on your case far more."

"I owe her."

"Take care of yourself, Vik. Love you. Call me soon."

She hung up before I could respond, but I hated protracted goodbyes anyway. Amma had never been one to mince words.

For the next forty minutes, the hum of tires bore me down the highway, toward Pineville. Katelyn worked until closing today, which meant I'd definitely stop in to see her. Once in town, I parked, stepped inside the local Outfitters store, and gazed around.

A rush of air conditioning blasted my face, smelling like new t-shirts and squeaky clean tennis shoes. Behind the counter, a man with graying hair and strong arms waved.

"Vik. Back here."

Daniel, owner of this store and a sister one in Jackson City, beckoned me closer. He wore an ancient fishing vest, decorated with lures and a name tag that said *Old Hoss*. He'd been wearing it since I was in high school and I sincerely hoped it hadn't been that long since it was washed. He held out a hand, shaking mine, as I approached. His salt-and-pepper hair jostled under a fan that whirred behind him.

"Thanks for coming." His hazel eyes brightened. "Good to see you again."

"Same, Hoss."

Daniel leaned his hands on the counter. "So, you want a job?"

"I'm thinking about it."

"We need some part-time help." With an arched eyebrow, he gestured to my knee. "Doesn't really look like you're up for that just yet."

"I will be in three weeks. Brace comes off next week."

Daniel hummed under his breath. "Just need some more hands over the summer to run the place. Mostly fill-in work on the register." He waved a vague hand over piles of clothes and gear. "That sort of thing."

I blinked. "Any lifting?"

"Not really. Just counter stuff. Iesha can get the rest, she likes to do stocking and inventory."

"If you can wait three weeks, I'll take it."

"Great." He slapped the glass countertop. "It's yours."

I laughed. "You don't want to interview me or something?"

He canted an eyebrow. "Do I need to?"

"Not as far as I'm concerned."

Daniel rolled his eyes. "I've known you your whole life. Your father and I fished together for a decade before they moved. I trust you, Vik. Plus, this store isn't that hard to run, and you're a smart guy." He straightened. "No alcohol, no drugs."

I held up two hands.

"Sober for three months now."

A swift nod followed.

While working at the Outfitters wasn't my number one job of choice, it was simple, got me out of my place, and involved the outdoors. In other words—a step forward. After wallowing for too many months, I needed a win.

Desperately.

The discount on gear would be welcome, not to mention the contact with great guides, and a little money coming in. Proximity to Kate was the sugar syrup on the gulab jamun, so to speak.

"When do you want me to start?" I asked.

"I'll call you a week before. We're transitioning a few other people out, anyway. Three weeks should work."

A bell on the door clanged, admitting a stooped male with dingy blonde hair. He gave a surly chin lift and wound his way through a few clothing racks. Something about him seemed familiar. A kid from high school, probably.

Daniel tilted his head to the side, gaze tapered on the man.

"Interesting."

"You know him?" I asked, rooting in my pocket for my car keys.

"Timothy Hanover. Just got released from prison, I hear."

"Huh."

Daniel shook his head, voice low. "Tough family life growing up. Things went bad for him five years ago, I hear, and he went to jail. Parents died while he was in there, too. Didn't know he'd gotten out. Anyway, see you in the morning."

Daniel slapped my back and stepped into the store. Relieved to have an excuse to get out of my apartment, and eyeballing a new standup paddle board along the far wall, I escaped the Outfitters.

Time to visit Katelyn.

Chapter Eleven

KATELYN

The rush of summer tourists breezed through the Frolicking Moose, which kept the hours steadily ticking by. I manned the espresso machine, scooped ice, called out orders, and enjoyed the waves of heat that came in the drive-through window after a chilly winter.

While crowds of people on their way to the reservoir occupied my attention, Bastian sat in the corner with his computer and an iced coffee at his fingertips. In the months that I'd worked here, he'd spoken less than fifteen words to me. He always had a brief smile, one that turned megawatt and steamy when Dahlia caught his eye with a sassy smirk.

On the other hand, Dahlia never stopped talking.

His presence helped me feel safe, however, so I never questioned it. According to Dahlia, this was his first summer not working as a wildland firefighter. Instead, he tapped away on a computer, doing who-knew-what.

In a temporary customer lull, I leaned against the counter and reoriented my brain. My thoughts drifted to Vikram, but I firmly yanked them back. No, I thought about him enough at home. I didn't need to give him more mental space here.

Bastian perked up.

"There's trouble," he rumbled.

Dahlia and I whipped around to look outside. In the parking lot, Vik approached. His long hair flowed around his shoulders. He'd shaven, and the hollows of his cheeks looked soft, just waiting for his stubble to creep back in. Aviator sunglasses hid his eyes.

I. Wanted. To. Die.

Dahlia passed by behind me, murmuring under her breath, "Why," she whispered, "is he so gorgeous?"

"To eternally torment me," I mumbled.

She laughed.

Hot air raced inside with him when he stepped through the doors. He yanked off his glasses, smiled at me, gave Bastian a chin lift, and strode to the counter with minimal limping from his left leg. His progress seemed to improve every day.

"Hey lady," he murmured, eyes on the chalkboard. "What's good?"

The word *lady* caught my stomach. I forced myself to breathe through a rush of butterflies. It was Appa's favorite nickname for Amma. The effortless way Vikram said it made me think he wasn't even aware he'd assigned it to me.

"Ah, everything?" I gulped, then said more confidently, "Everything is good. The passionfruit tea is the special this week. I think you'd like it. It's a mixture of green-and-black teas, with passionfruit syrup."

Dahlia bounced to my side in a tank top with a picture of her home island, Tonga, across the front. She studied Vik with a practiced, critical eye.

"I got this, Vik!" she said confidently. "Matching people with their drinks is my superpower. You would enjoy a large green tea, double bagged, with creamer and cane sugar, because you don't do artificial, but not too much of either, because you're also a purist. Iced, of course, because it's friggin' hot outside."

A huge smile wreathed his face.

"On point, Dahlia, as always."

She brushed her shoulders off. "It's what I do."

Across the way, Bastian sent her an air high-five. She winked, and he sent her a look that suggested he'd devour her if she stepped too close.

"Coming right up," I said to Vik.

He tossed a ten on the counter, his gaze steady on me. I wanted to shiver under the heat of his stare.

"How's the day?" he asked.

"Not too bad."

He lit up. "I got a job at the Outfitters, by the way."

"Congrats!"

"I start in three weeks. Should be just right. I'm ready to be out of the house."

Dahlia whistled and threw a napkin in the air. Vik bowed slightly at the waist while I slung his tea together, being overly generous with my favorite creamer. It wasn't healthy, but with any luck, he wouldn't inquire. I had a hunch he'd love it against the notes of green.

The ice cubes clinked together when I set it in front of him. He reached for it, but didn't go anywhere. With no one else stepping into the shop, he stayed. His eyes hadn't left me. I squirmed, both self-conscious and delighted by the full power of his stare.

How many times had I dreamed of such a moment as this?

Was it real?

Did I imagine a note of interest in his heady perusal?

"Are you excited about the Outfitters?" I asked to get out of my own head.

"Yes. Daniel is pretty chill. It'll be the perfect summer job to get me through physical therapy, until I figure out what's next."

Bastian snorted.

Vik narrowed his eyes on him.

"Will you work every day?" I asked, and grabbed a washcloth to wipe down the counter, just to have something to do with my hands. Otherwise, I might reach over, grab that attractive face, and smack his lips to mine.

"Through the summer," he murmured, "I hope so."

Secretly, I couldn't help a rush of relief. Vik in close proximity could only make me feel safer, as selfish as such a thing seemed. I'd already overtaken his house for the past week or so, but this seemed just right.

"Can you sit with me for a minute?" he asked, reaching for the tall, plastic cup. Before I could respond, Dahlia shoved me away from the counter, bouncing my hip with hers to get me moving.

"You bet she can! It's her break time."

Vik winked at her. To me, he said, "Then let's go outside, lady. It's gorgeous."

Full summer sun descended on the porch outside, drawing the scent of warmed pine into the air. Waves of heat basking off the asphalt wrinkled the air. A wiry metal table, painted white, sat off to the side with two chairs propped next to it. An open umbrella shaded it from the heat. I lowered into one of the chairs. Vik moved his so it closed the space between us, but faced the mountains. His sunglasses slid back over his eyes, and I breathed easier.

Splashing, and a squeal, came from behind the coffee shop, where the gentle waves of the lake lingered not far away.

"Do you have any fun summer plans?" He had a pull of the tea, held it in his mouth a moment, then swallowed. A quick grin appeared there. "Perfect."

A snort almost escaped me.

"Summer plans? Ah, no."

An inquiring eyebrow raised. He tilted the iced tea toward

me, outstretched in a silent offer. I hesitated, but accepted. The cool notes of green tea, creamy and slightly sweet, cooled my throat in the heat.

"Thanks."

He winked. "You say *no* as if that should have been an obvious thing. Why don't you have any fun summer plans?"

"Money has been tight, so I've been planning on picking up any extra hours that I can. I'm trying to save up to go see Vini after the baby comes."

Plus, I added, *I don't have anywhere to go except Vini and new places are too frightening and I think I forgot how.*

Those words remained locked away. Rules number one and four made a clear delineation in this regard: never alone, never somewhere new by myself. With no family that I was close to—or would want to visit—and Vini so far away, little captured my interest.

Or so I told myself.

Traveling alone, after a lifetime of my best friend glued to my hip, had always felt empty anyway. After the assault, too overwhelming. New places made it difficult to feel safe, and I ended up locking myself in a hotel as soon as darkness hinted on the horizon.

I'd tried.

It didn't work.

Vik made a noise in his throat. He leaned back, the picture of casual ease, and crossed his right ankle across his uninjured knee. He peered out on the mountains, hints of the lake sparkling in the background. My gaze wandered to his well-sculpted calves, the ease of his flip flops and simple shorts. The man could wear burlap and I'd find him the sexiest person on the planet.

"No fun plans for me either," he murmured. "That's sad, because summer is the best. Ripe with opportunities for crazy things."

"Your forté," I quipped.

He laughed, gesturing to his leg with a flippant wave. "This makes it difficult, for sure. But yes, crazy things are a speciality of mine."

"You obviously have thoughts."

He flashed a quick grin. "I do."

"And they are?" I drawled.

"What if we figure out some fun things to do together?"

"Like what?"

He shrugged. "Anything. At this point, I've been holed up in my apartment for too long. I need sunshine, adventure, and people. The job will help but . . . I'm bored."

My heart raced at the thought of planning something with Vikram, even if borne from boredom. I'd take any opportunity to spend time with him, as a pseudo-little-sister, tenant, or old family friend.

"With you," I heard myself say, "I'm up for anything."

Heat blossomed through my cheeks. Could I reveal my cards any more clearly than that? Did he notice the purl of warmth in the tone that I had no way of pulling back? My response to Vikram was a study of wild things. Control one second, none the next. He brought an erratic side out of me that I'd once loved.

Absent-mindedly, he passed the tea my way. I had a long pull this time, letting the cold drink center me back into reality. Away from the spicy flutters of heat that shot through me every time he spoke. When I handed it back, his fingers wrapped around mine. My breath caught. He paused, glanced at me with interest, and held it.

A thousand years seemed to pass.

Too soon—but after far too long at the same time—the warmth of his fingers slipped away. My heart banged around my throat in reckless flails as I leaned back, cleared my throat, and attempted to pull myself together. I set the drink aside, unable to wrap my thoughts around drinking it.

Ho-leee coconuts.

This man.

Wordless, we remained on the porch for another five minutes. The butterflies in my stomach slowed. My clenched body unwound. A morsel at a time, I wrestled my thoughts back under control.

"I should go back to work," I said, standing. Vik smiled up at me.

"Thanks, Kate. See you tonight?"

All the awkwardness melted away. Crush, brother-to-my-best-friend, or something else, Vikram was, above all, my friend.

"Tonight."

His eyes followed me all the way in, and lingered long after I left.

* * *

Kinoshi, town attorney for Pineville, stared at me from over the top of a glossy desk. He had a perpetually kind expression and dimpled cheeks. The professional-chic feel of his space, with neatly stacked papers, black-and-white decorations, and a cool hit of peppermint, put me at ease.

"Most judges are going to move a restraining order like this through the system pretty quickly," he said as he closed a manilla folder in front of him. "In cases of sexual assault, they typically don't dawdle. In fact, I think we could have a permanent restraining order in place within two weeks."

I sank back against the chair. Two weeks was better than I expected. With any luck, I could stay with Vik without having to reveal why I didn't want to leave. The words, *I've loved you my whole life and now I love you too much to stay* just didn't quite hit the mark.

"That's excellent news," I said with a sigh. "Timothy was released last week, and I haven't seen any sign of him so far."

"Also a good sign."

I cleared my throat. "What if he tried to find me or follow me or something before the restraining order is in effect?"

"We can escalate to an emergent one."

Some of my miserable fear chipped away a little. The gauzy protection of a restraining order wasn't as physically strong as the walls of a prison, but it gave me the sense of doing *something*.

Would paper stop a man like Timothy?

Or was I the only one that hadn't forgotten? Timothy had spent the last five years wallowing in prison. He'd either built up an intense hatred against me for putting him there or . . .

He'd moved on.

Maybe I needed to as well.

Until I knew for certain, all was conjecture. The flailing uncertainty is what prodded my rampant anxieties the most.

Kinoshi smiled gently, and the action reminded me of how supportive he'd been when I first approached him, traumatized, but determined to act. Vinita and Amma had held me up the whole time, one on either side. Sometimes physically held me up. At the time, I felt like a torn flower petal. Weak. Fragile.

Crushed.

But I came back.

"Of course, there's no way to physically enforce the restraining order at first," Kinoshi continued, as if he sensed my brewing questions, "but it does give you recourse with the law if he attempts to come near you or contact you. While on parole, the rules are more strict and would work in your favor with a restraining order. Local authorities can escalate a situation and he could return to jail if he attempts to do so. It's a boundary that, if he crosses, has ramifications."

"It's something, I guess."

He shuffled through some paperwork. "Take this home, fill

it out, and you can drop it off at my office when you're done. I'll start to put everything together for the petition to the judge, and we'll take it from there."

The manilla file folder shuffled across the top of the desk, and I leaned forward to accept it. The thickness startled me—there was more paperwork to it than I thought. Filling all those boxes and lines out gave me a sense of dread—just his name brought back thoughts and memories I'd rather not deal with again—but Vinita's voice in my mind soothed me.

You feel and you deal.

With a deep breath, I pressed my thumb into my palm. The action anchored me into warm memories of Vinita, Amma, Appa, and . . . Vikram. The simple movement brought me out of the quick spiral of terror, as it always had.

If I were honest with myself? Vikram did that more than the trained physical clue. Knowing he was on my side—without knowing the stakes—made me feel far less alone. More able to deal with the ups and downs this world provided.

At this point, I'd take whatever worked.

"Thank you," I said, meeting Kinoshi's inquiring gaze. "I can't tell you what it means to have your help and your speed."

He stood, offering a hand. "I'm always here for you. No charge for the restraining order of course. I know it can be scary and overwhelming, and you don't technically need a lawyer to do this. I just want you to know that we're on your side."

Tears prickled in my eyes. "Thank you, Kinoshi. That means more than you could ever know."

His warm smile escorted me out of the office, folder tucked under my arm. The warm sunshine beat on my shoulders, heating them gently. Trucks sped by, towing boats. The sound of distant four wheelers rang in the air. My stomach growled, hungry despite the plate of breakfast Vikram had left for me in the morning with a note that said, *Enjoy.*

Kinoshi's kind, reserved face laid to rest some of the building fear that had accumulated inside me. The sunshine dispelled the rest.

A text message dinged on my phone, and my traitorous heart leaped at the thought that it might be Vik. The escalating beat calmed when I saw the name.

Bethany: Hey chica! I've been browsing listings every morning and evening and haven't seen any new rentals pop up. I'll keep an eye out and let you know.

Katelyn: Thank you! I'll keep an eye peeled as well.

Bethany: There *are* places available, but not anything that I'd want a single woman being part of. We'll get you something safe and affordable, I know it. It just takes awhile when you stay in the mountains.

Her last comment sent a frisson of uncertainty through me. Why *did* I stay in the mountains?

Why not move somewhere else? I could be a barista at any coffee shop, so what was the draw to stay here?

The answer had been easy only a few months ago. Pineville was home. The thought of re-establishing myself somewhere new felt just as overwhelming as Timothy's return. Here, at least, I knew people. They knew me. In a small town, safety lurked around every corner. In a new place?

Not at all.

The idea of leaving swamped me with further uncertainty. I'd rather surround myself with familiarity than branch out before I knew whether Timothy even thought of me anymore.

Vikram changed all of that.

Besides, I'd grown up here. Sure, I'd left for a few years to wriggle my way through college with a degree I didn't care about now, then lived next to Vinita for a few years while I gained my courage back, but I hadn't felt safe until I returned.

With a shake of my head, I sent those thoughts away, pressed my thumb into my palm, and thought of Vini. Instead of Vini, Vikram surfaced, and the desired sense of peace followed in a flood. His home. The locked doors. The sound of his humming while he fixed curry.

I'm safe, I reminded myself.

For the first time, it felt like it.

Between Bethany Mercedy looking for new places to rent on the real estate side, and Dahlia asking every single local that came into the shop, *something* was bound to pop up. Something protected and long-term and accompanied by a solid contract, at any rate.

I slipped into my car, closed the door, locked it, and let out a long breath. Getting that meeting with Kinoshi over felt like a step in the right direction. Like I'd done something to . . . move forward.

Create safety.

That was the thing about safety, though. You spent a lifetime trying to cultivate it, and a split-second decision controlled by someone else broke *all* that work.

Didn't I know it?

Another text rang on my phone, pulling me from my thoughts.

Vikram: Chicken Biryani tonight.

My lips twitched into a smile.

Katelyn: Keep it from being too dry?

Vikram: Don't offend me.

Feeling a great deal more vibrant, I set my phone aside, clicked on my seatbelt, and drove away from Kinoshi's. For now, I'd done everything I could do. I was on my way to a safe house where I lived with the love of my life—though he didn't know that—and tonight I would sleep more peacefully than I had in years.

Life was good.

* * *

A rock song accompanied me home.

I let the loud music swell through the speakers, banging in my head. It wasn't often that I listened to music in the car. The drone of music and voices and noise in the coffee shop all day normally left me desperate for quiet, but today I didn't want to think. I just wanted some other oblivion to crowd my thoughts.

Once I stopped at Vikram's, I put my car into park, leaned my head back against the headrest, and closed my eyes. Drum solo notwithstanding, my thoughts surfaced through the chaos anyway.

I've got this, I told myself. *I can go in there, be casual with him, hide the restraining order, and not fall deeper in love.*

Who am I kidding?

I couldn't love him more than I do now.

The song ended, shaking me from my stupor. I turned the car off, grabbed my purse, the file of papers, and headed inside. The smell of roasted chicken, and a cool sweep of air conditioning, welcomed me inside. Vikram's head popped out from around the corner. He brightened into a smile.

"Hey."

"Hey," I replied, then closed the door, locked it, and set my purse on a hook in the wall. "Dinner smells so good."

He disappeared as he snorted.

I closed my eyes and inhaled deeply, but held the restraining order paperwork close to my chest. That was something he didn't need to know about.

Ever.

If I could get away with it.

"Get changed if you want," he called, still out of sight, "it'll be ready in just a few minutes."

A giddy sense of relief replaced the weight of my day. Dinner with Vikram was not only delicious, but also better than a show. The way his smile illuminated his eyes. The play of muscles when he moved. He joked easily, so naturally charming, that when it was the two of us I could almost see something dancing between us.

Something I'd only harbored in my dreams.

After shucking off my work clothes, changing into a pair of shorts and a t-shirt, and sliding into a pair of flip flops, I wandered into the kitchen. Pans littered the top of the range. Sizzling vegetables off to the side. Strips of chicken—perfectly marinated and cooked. Shreds of onion skin littered the countertop near grains of rice. Vikram might be perfectly neat in everywhere else, but he unleashed his inner monster in the kitchen.

He glanced up and gave me a warm, full-bodied smile. My stomach dropped all the way to my toes.

Sweet baby pineapple.

How did he do that?

"Smells delicious," I managed. He grinned, that white-toothed smile that had always captured me.

I slipped to the other side of him and reached for plates out of the cupboard. Otherwise, I'd gawk and drool and never recover my pride. We fell easily into our routine. He happily slaved over delicious food; I set the table. The workload was way out of balance in my favor, but I'd take it all day.

"Do you still like to watch movies?" he asked, breaking a run of quiet. I jumped, startled when his voice came from just behind me. "Oh, sorry. I didn't mean to scare you."

"You didn't!" I said too quickly. "I just . . . I didn't know you were there."

He reached around my side, setting a bowl of rice on the table. Spices graced the top in a bright sheen. His scent wafted past, paralyzing me. I swallowed hard, arrested by a brush of warmth. His skin almost met mine.

Tantalizingly close.

My heart clumsily recovered from the near-touch. Or was it the startle? I couldn't be sure.

"So," he drawled. "Movies?"

"Ah, movies? Yes. I like movies."

A skein of incredulousness filled his voice. "The Korean monster movies that Vini used to be obsessed with?"

Unable to help myself, I laughed. "Those will forever be a favorite."

"Well, I grabbed a few rentals online earlier today if you want to watch with me. I thought about going out but . . ."

He trailed away, then reached for the chicken. Vikram, like his father, was a perceptive figure. He acted like he didn't see everything, but he absorbed each detail. I couldn't dismiss the thought that he'd noticed how little I ventured into the world. Did he rent the movies instead of going to the theater because of me?

The thought that I'd eventually have to tell him about Timothy ran through my mind. Didn't I owe him that much? If I found another place to stay, the need to inform him would no longer exist. Frankly, it wouldn't be his business then. I couldn't dismiss whether I owed it to him now, though. I was about to file for a protective restraining order against a man who committed sexual assault.

Yes. I owed my roommate that information.

But *I* had been that assault victim, and the thought of saying those words to someone like Vikram broke me apart inside. Vik was a good man, but even the best of men would have questions. Concerns. They'd wonder. They'd see me differently.

After finally feeling safe again, could I do it?

The hope that I'd find a new, safe place to stay rushed up to save me. When I found that place, I'd tell him then. That way, if it became weird between us, he'd have an out. He wouldn't have to face me every day with whatever reaction or response he had.

"I'd love to watch movies with you," I said when I realized I'd fallen quiet for too long. "I haven't been out to a new movie in years, though. If you wanted to go to the theater, I'd be interested in that as well."

His dark brows rose. "Really?"

Hesitation stole back over me. Dark theater? Ah, no thanks. Unpredictable shadows. People milling around. Unless you sat at the back, you had nothing firm behind you. The exits were far away. The rules let out a riotous squeal of protest. They didn't like this idea. Rule two—never in the dark—and seven—never go on a date alone—in particular.

I shook myself out of that spiral.

No.

This wasn't the scary, made-up world that existed in my head, always ready to kill me. This was a movie with Vikram, of all people. Recovering from surgery or not, there was no one else in the world that would keep me safer. Our earlier conversation about summer, and my embarrassing lack of *fun* plans, pushed me further into the nudge.

How long had it been since I'd stepped foot in a movie theater, anyway? Time for some healthy boundary changes.

"Yeah," I said with more conviction. "I'd really enjoy that. Especially today."

"Today? Did something happen?"

Realizing my slip, I waved a hand with a laugh. "Oh, no. Just . . . it would be nice to have a change of scenery, that's all."

A huge grin split his face. "Then let's do it. There's a fantastic new monster movie playing in two hours. We have time to eat, leave the mess, and head over. You down?"

I returned the smile, eager for a new adventure.

One that felt so safe.

"Let's do it."

* * *

The last movie that I'd gone into a dark theater to watch had been an animated one, two weeks before Timothy assaulted me. The low lights, escape into the screen, and swelling soundtrack had been so fun.

About a year after Timothy's assault, I attempted moviegoing again. The room felt too dark, the walls too close, the strangers too near. I sat in my chair for all of thirty seconds, then strolled right back out.

I hadn't returned.

Tonight, my entire body tightened in anticipation of a narrowing reaction. The fright in my chest. Fluttering stomach. Clammy hands. Darting eyes. Yet . . . none showed. Only a gentle burr in my chest, a discomfort. I attributed the lack of anxiety to the powerful shoulders at my side, the warm curl of Vikram's voice right next to me.

"Monster movies are so much more advanced these days," he tutted under his breath. "Let me know if you get freaked out. They put what you and Vini used to watch into preschool."

I scoffed.

He laughed.

His credit card captured both our tickets. Before I could protest, he silenced me with a look that reminded me so much of Appa, I laughed. The tips of his fingers guided the small of my back as we navigated the theater. Our arms brushed with every third or fourth step. He remained at my side, a stolid presence that banished all of those other thoughts.

For the first time in a while, I breathed freely in public.

The theater smelled like overheated popcorn and red-hots. The whir and hiss of a soda machine, along with the distant wail of a baby, bounced around the walls. I gazed around the almost empty place, my arm brushing lightly against his again. Chills slipped all the way through me.

"Hardly anyone is here," I murmured, relieved for the open space. Not only did it make it easier to watch for Timothy in case he popped up, but to canvas for other threats. Vikram looked around, startled, as if he hadn't noticed.

"Should be a quiet night."

With a gentle touch, he put a hand on my elbow to turn me into the right theater. My stomach quivered, though he let go as soon as I followed. He hovered close, always close enough to touch. Vik had always been that way. I'd been able to convince myself that it didn't mean anything—the man would cuddle with a rock, given the chance—but tonight I *wanted* the fluttering caresses to mean something.

"Well," he murmured as we emerged from the tunnel into the showroom "Look at that. All to ourselves."

Relief weakened me.

"The rule for every monster movie," he said as he started up the low-slung stairs, "is to sit in the very middle."

"Why the middle?"

"So you aren't tempted to leave in shame and humiliation and fright, of course. You will be cajoled if you leave."

I snorted.

"Leaving is for wimps."

"You speak so confidently," he sang, shooting me a wink. "But I'm telling you, this monster movie is something else. Just real enough to be totally creepy."

My hesitation had far less to do with the Hollywood-made

monsters on the screen, and everything to do with the hulk of a man that I wanted to wrap in my arms and never let go. The sort of monster that Vikram inspired in my life was a different kind of horror movie altogether.

Vikram wouldn't take kindly to me pasting my body to his, I would imagine.

Or maybe . . .

I stopped that thought as soon as it came. That was one tree I had no business barking up. At least, in monster movies, I didn't have to worry about romance. Sappy love scenes. Watching a tender first kiss between two lovers while Vikram lounged at my side might rob all my air.

While tired advertisements shuffled through the screen, I quizzed Vik on his top ten ranking of monster movies, starting with country of origin and B-rank status. Plenty of guffaws, challenges, and laughs later, the lights dimmed until they turned off. Unable to help it, my muscles clenched. I pressed my middle finger to my palm, let out a deep breath, thought of Vini, and molded into the seat.

More quickly than usual, the discomfort began to fade. Vik placed his arm against mine on the rest and the warm touch of his skin melted away the uncertainty.

The movie flashed by in subdued tones at first, a story about a girl and her best friend in a creepy forest. Lost, they wandered in fog, stalked by an animal that wasn't quite earthly. During a predictable—but still shocking—jump scare, I squeaked and grabbed the chair arm. Vik's hand instantly clamped around mine, secure and reassuring. Heat flooded my cheeks, but embarrassment faded into the dizzying allure of his warm palm. The long, strong fingers.

His touch whisked my breath away. I didn't even have room to scream when a half-bear, half-humanoid monster appeared from the shadows and bit the best friend's face off in a putrid *crunch* of bone.

My air had been taken.

Stolen.

I gave it so willingly.

While Vik chuckled over an equally grisly closing scene where the remaining girl killed the monster with a knife buried all the way into its gurgling throat, I sat there like a beating heart, all thuds. Pounds. Blasts. Vikram grabbed my hand—then didn't let go for over half an hour now. Alerts flashed like a ticker tape through my mind.

Warning.

Warning.

Warning.

No, I told the frightened voice. *This is different.*

Vikram wasn't a violent approach. No sneak attack in the dark, rainy night. Vikram simply held my hand to provide a tender comfort. A glance at his profile revealed a man absorbed in a monster movie, which hardly classified the hand-holding as something special. He'd probably forgotten.

His touchy nature, kindness to me, and brotherly protectiveness created a formula that looked and felt like interest, but couldn't possibly be.

Fool's gold.

Only I wouldn't be the fool again.

As the credits ran across the screen, I surreptitiously untangled our fingers as I pretended to stretch. He glanced over, one hand held up in question.

"Well?" he drawled.

My already-wrung out heart managed one last gasp of agonized disbelief at his natural beauty.

"Three out of five stars," I quipped through a yawn, hoping to cover the strangled sound. He tilted his head back and laughed. I looked away, far too tempted to run my fingers down his neck.

"Too predictable?"

"They all are," I said with a wider smile that might have appeared a bit *too* forced. The lights flickered back to low lumination, revealing a couple ahead of us that snuck in during the opening credits. The woman stood, glanced up, then did a fast double-take. Even in the dim theater, I could see the brightness of a pristine smile.

"Vik?"

Vik straightened like an interested cat. He blinked, peered at her, and smiled. A strange tightness overtook his face. His casual mien didn't fool me, because I knew the real Vikram.

Whatever washed over him was someone else altogether.

"Blanca?"

The lovely girl beamed, murmured something to the male at her side, and headed down the row. Vikram followed, walking away from me, and they met in a friendly hug on the stairs. The other man lifted an eyebrow, his neck tight.

Feeling awkward—and way too aware of Vik's hand lingering on Blanca's shoulder—I gathered my jacket and slid my arms inside. My gaze diverted away from them as he laughed. I shuffled through my purse, praying for a text message to distract me.

Something.

Anything.

Another laugh pealed out from the stairs, where Blanca pressed a hand to her chest. "Oh," she cried, "you always made me laugh."

Desperate *not* to hear, I scrambled for any reason to get out of there without looking like a jealous psychopath.

Nothing came to my rescue.

"It's been awhile," Blanca murmured more quietly. "How have you been, Vik?"

A false note of brightness infused his tone. "Nothing too exciting for me. How about you?"

"Just moved back home for a bit. My Mom is sick."

"I'm sorry."

Blanca's head tilted, cascading glossy hair to the side. Her lips pursed in a pouty, sad gesture. "It's been rough."

"I'll send out good vibes for her."

C'mon, Vini! I thought. *Send me a text! Why don't you call?*

Not a single message appeared on my phone. No emails. Why couldn't spam callers ring when it would be advantageous, like right now? Then I could escape with a plausible reason that didn't taste like egregious envy. That ugly, green, creeping monster, far more destructive than any of the beasts in monster movies.

"Thanks." Blanca sighed. "I appreciate that. It's always nice to get out of the house and away from it for a bit, even for a scary movie with way too much blood and gore."

She tacked on a too-high laugh. Her date put a hand on her back, his other tucked into his jean pockets. He eyed Vikram. I turned my back and rummaged through my purse without seeing a thing.

"Are you still driving the trains?" Blanca asked.

"Not right now. Switched to something else."

"That's Vik." Another false laugh. "Always moving, always shifting onto the next exciting thing."

The bitterness in those words definitely *wasn't* my imagination. Neither was the blatant desperation, thwarted love, in her too-wide eyes. Like she scrambled to hold onto something slippery, ethereal, uncatchable.

Wasn't that Vik?

Slippery.

Uncatchable.

What was I doing here? What had I been thinking? I'd combined safety and my lifelong love for Vikram up together, and blurred the safe lines my rules provided. This was dangerous ground, as shaky as anything I'd ever stood on before. Like living on a fault line. I'd have no one to blame but myself when the pain returned.

Frantic now, because I'd be expected to join them next, I clicked through my phone settings, picked the right spot, and tapped on the screen. A sample phone ring trilled into the air, loud against a sudden quiet spell. I feigned surprise and silenced it by pretending to answer a call that wasn't real.

Vikram's voice quieted behind me as I flung my purse over my shoulder and became engrossed in a fake conversation. With a hand held out in both greeting and apology, I hustled down the hallway and threw myself through the double doors. The glaring lights in the foyer calmed my alarm enough to think.

Why was I panicking? Vikram being around an interested girl was hardly news.

I couldn't be having an attack.

Not here.

Timothy wasn't in sight. I felt safe. Plenty of lights and people and . . . why did it feel so suffocating?

So . . . frightening?

Because Blanca was a deft reminder that Vikram didn't live the life I wanted. Commitment made him laugh, or scoff. I'd let myself fall even harder for a man that I couldn't capture. It's like I brought the pain to myself.

The constriction around my chest increased, like a ratchet twisted from the inside out. The bathroom doors slammed open when I shoved through, found a stall, and locked it behind me. The cool metal pressed against my cheek reoriented me. I screwed my eyes shut.

"Vini," I whispered. "Vini. Vini. Vini."

Focusing on my best friend, my stable star, brought me out of the sheer panic. Deep breaths, low and slow and filling, helped the wild edge abate. Sense returned a half-breath at a time, until all my fragmented thoughts slowed.

Vikram may not be the committing type, but neither of us

had asked for commitment. Besides, I'd been in love with him all my life and survived. How could now be any different?

I pressed my back to the stall and closed my eyes.

"Get it together," I murmured. "Go back out there, smile, go home with Vik, and go to bed. This won't look so bleak in the morning."

After a few more long breaths, I slipped out, splashed some cold water on my face, and pulled myself back together. Vikram could talk to all the women he wanted—former lovers, dates, friends. It wouldn't matter to me anymore.

Until Vik said the words, *I want you to be mine,* then we would remain what we'd always been.

Friends.

And I could learn to accept that.

Heart heavy, I returned to the foyer. A subdued Vikram lounged against a wall, forehead furrowed in deep lines. I squared my shoulders.

Reminders.

That's what happened tonight.

Blanca was a good reminder that playing with fire led to getting burned.

* * *

The rigid walls of the Pineville grocery store surrounded Dahlia and me with baked goods and canned jellies, some tied with a blue-ribbon reminder from a county fair ten years ago. A "business meeting" with a woman named Priyanka had drawn Bastian away until who-knew-when. Without him constantly haunting the corner of the Frolicking Moose, full-force Dahlia bounced around the shop and my love life.

"So . . ."

Dahlia peered at me, eyes wide. Her long, dark lashes

blinked, fanning against her cheeks before opening again. Eagerness filled such a gaze.

I sighed.

"You want to talk about Vik."

"Yes!" she cried, so loud it was almost a scream. "Please! Can we please talk about this? Leslie won't admit it, but she loves being the barista. She can run it while we get milk and ice and chat."

"The only reason I'm entertaining this conversation," I said with a long tone of warning, "is because your boyfriend isn't walking across the street with us."

She squealed, clapping. "Spill it! Tell me from the very beginning of when you met him to now. *Everything.*"

We headed toward the dairy section at the back of the grocery store. I canvassed the room, spotted all the visible people, and kept going without a hitch. If there was any skill I had fully adopted, it was scanning an area for potential threats.

Rule nine: never unaware.

"Vikram and I grew up together," I said, eyebrows high. "Which is where it started. Like, when I was ten or eleven, all right? It's not a big deal. He's . . ."

The words *like a big brother to me* tripped on my tongue. While true, it also wasn't true. No sister would feel this way about a brother. Like she'd tripped on stars and couldn't stop falling.

"A friend?" Dahlia supplied.

"Ah . . ."

That word didn't quite peg it either.

Vikram was safety, not just friendship . . . but he was *also* friendship. The fun, flirty, happy side of things that so rarely came together in a boyfriend. Somehow, I knew that nothing could touch me when he lingered near. Vik was . . . comfort.

Companionship.

A deeper part of my soul.

That *deeper part of my soul* was currently slumming around at his townhouse after an awkward car ride home at the theater nights ago. After that, neither of us had much to say. I crept out of the house half an hour early and stayed at the shop late to be certain to avoid him for the last couple of days.

Like a total coward.

"He's my best friend's brother," I continued, oriented back into the moment when Dahlia reached for a carton of full-fat milk. "His sister, Vinita, was my best friend and my world growing up. We were inseparable until college. She moved out to New York with her husband and is pregnant right now. I lived with her for a few years and moved back last year. His parents are like my parents. They buy me plane tickets to see them at Christmas and Amma calls me all the time."

Dahlia leaned back. "Sounds like a perfect romance! The whole older-brother-next-door kind of best friend thing? I love that plot line. Sweet baby pineapple, but Jess should do that one next!"

I groaned. "Please don't start talking about that romance author you're obsessed with. You know that's not real life."

"It's more real than you think," Dahlia muttered, but covered the sound with a blithe smile. "Look, this is about you. You lit up like a Christmas tree when he stepped in the shop the other day. I saw it. You have to be feeling something."

My lips parted to protest, but I slammed them shut again. The color drained from my face. I stared at her, horrified.

Was I *that* transparent?

"Do you think he can tell?" I whispered.

Dahlia squealed again.

"Confirmation!" she cried, one hand in the air, the other clutching the gallon of milk. She set it on the ground impatiently, hands flapping. "You *do* have a thing for him. I mean, who wouldn't? He's so beautiful. Also, no. I don't think he notices anything at all. He's a bit too rummy with his *own* eyes on you. Believe it or not, he returns it. Boy's got the hots for you!"

"That is totally impossible."

Dahlia reared back like I'd slapped her. "Excuse you? How is that impossible? You're amazing, Katelyn. You have this demure look with your glasses, but then you're super snappy when you actually speak."

Snappy?

What did *that* mean?

Before I could ask, movement from an aisle behind Dahlia caught my eye. One moment I sputtered over how to reply to such a statement, and the next all the blood squeezed from my body.

A figure slunk toward the deli section, slightly hunched. Hands in pockets, head down. He had light hair and a frown that appeared perpetual. Black shirt, black jeans.

Black soul.

His eyes fluttered up and locked on mine.

I gasped.

Timothy straightened, clearly startled to see me. He froze, hand outstretched toward a package of ground meat. Tattoos scrawled across his knuckles now, I couldn't recall them before. His shoulders dropped and eyes widened.

"You okay?" Dahlia asked. "You're so pale all of a sudden. Kate?"

Timothy shifted toward me, an unreadable expression on his face. In it, I saw pain. Frustration.

Intensity.

I flipped my back to him, in a mental panic.

Dahlia glanced over her shoulder. Her gaze lingered on Timothy for only a moment before returning to me with utter confusion. Timothy had always been the type that faded into the background. The sort of guy that you forgot as soon as you saw him, a threat written off.

How well I knew that.

Prison had changed him. He'd become a little stronger in the shoulders, but still lean. A granite-hard expression filled his face now.

Timothy was *angry*.

"Kate?" She stepped closer. "What's wrong?"

"Gotta go."

I ducked into the closest aisle and disappeared. Cereal boxes blurred past me as I jogged away, my chest tight. Tears prickled at my eyes as I spilled out of the other side, nearly crashing into someone. A pair of hands grabbed my shoulders to stop me from falling.

"Kate?"

Vikram peered at me, concern immediately evident. A light-headed feeling swept over me. His warm hands, gentle but firm, anchored me back in the moment. I put a hand on my chest.

"Can't . . . breathe."

Smooth as silk, he wrapped an arm around me and pulled me away. We ducked through swinging doors and into a back room. Freezers, cardboard boxes, and a few hand trucks littered the room. He pressed my back to a wall, stood in front of me like a shield, and braced one arm next to my face.

I couldn't see the store. Most importantly, no one in the store would see me. Finally, the locked tension in my chest gave way. I panted, desperate for breath.

His hand gently found my chin.

"Look at me, Kate."

The dizzy feeling abated when our eyes met. The closing black tunnel hovered with a prickling sensation on top of my scalp, and now I wasn't sure why I couldn't breathe.

Vik, or Timothy?

The smell of fresh shampoo drifted off Vik's damp strands, loose on his shoulders. I leaned back, grateful for the steady support, and pressed my thumbs to my palm. Unbidden, memories drifted through my mind. The gravel on my back. The empty parking lot. A vague scream that I'd later realize was my own.

This is exactly what I feared.

Violent history, restraining order, whatever else aside, this mountain town was too small for both me and Timothy. I'd run into him at every corner, every other moment. I couldn't go *anywhere*.

Couldn't live my life.

Vik's voice swam through the haze. I blinked, startled to see him still there. He put a warm hand on my face.

"I'm here, Kate. You're safe."

"Can't . . . breathe."

He sprawled his palm on my chest. "In," he murmured. I obeyed. "Hold." My chest stilled, filling with air and space and light. "Out." It rushed out of me, hungry to be free. Vikram's steady voice didn't waver. I grabbed his wrist, anchored.

"In," he commanded gently.

Then, as I'd been training for years, Vini surfaced in my mind. Amma and Appa. Vikram. Playing in the summer sunshine with sprinklers, dosas, and the smell of sandalwood incense heavy in the air. The goodness of my family—my real family—lay over the top of Timothy's terrible legacy.

Light surfaced again.

Safe.

My head realigned, my thoughts straightened out. The tightness began to fade, ebbing. Vik put his palm against my cheek. So gentle, so calm.

"Kate?"

Helpless, I could only stare. His rigid concern softened. He pulled me into his arms, encompassing and firm. I tucked my face into his neck with a pent-up sob. The muscles of his back elongated under my hands as he tightened his hold. His shirt caught my tears. His arms trapped my silent shaking. We stood in the backroom of the local grocery store with his body shielding mine.

Safe again.

But not really safe at all, because Vikram didn't belong to me.

Heart-pain or not, I couldn't let him go.

Chapter Twelve

VIKRAM

Hernandez: The guy you asked me about is Timothy Hanover. I remember him vaguely. He played on the JV football team. Used to give Grady problems. Our class. You remember him?

I glanced at the text, frowned, and responded. The guy at the outfitters ran back through my mind.
    That guy?

Vik: A little.

Hernandez: He was trouble in high school. Turns out he just got out of jail a few days ago.

    A dark feeling welled up in my gut.

Vik: Charges?

Hernandez: Sexual assault, five years back. You can find it online on the sex predators database.

Puzzle pieces slid together.

Katelyn's darting eyes. The panic attack in the coffee shop weeks ago. Her obsession with locking the house. The fear on her face when she'd been evicted, not to mention Vinita's vague warnings that alluded to something in her past. Her panic attack a few hours ago at the grocery store slid right into the ugliest puzzle I'd ever seen.

Now, I understood.

The urge to crush something rushed through me, hot as fire. I gripped my hand into a fist.

Bastard.

Bastard, bastard, bastard.

I jumped to my feet and paced, then sat back down. Whatever happened next, I had to get myself under control. She hadn't confirmed that Timothy had gone to jail for sexually assaulting *her*, but her reactions seemed to support the supposition. Particularly because Dahlia mentioned a guy standing behind them when the panic attack began.

A guy that fit Timothy's description.

I'd seen Kate go into the grocery store with Dahlia, laughing, moments before Timothy slunk in after her. That's when I'd followed, trailing a prickle of intuition that told me to get in there.

Technically, I was supposed to be home doing . . . something. Lunch with Kate, and clearing the weird air between us, had seemed a better alternative, which had taken me into Pineville.

Thank the universe.

Rage smoldered as I tried not to think too hard about it. My knuckles tightened. Fingers clenched. Kate would see my agitation. She might not feel safe or clam up or . . . something. Her endearing, occasional embarrassment and uncertainty was charming, but I wouldn't want her scared.

Not of me.

Not of anyone.

"Dammit," I muttered, running a hand through my hair.

The thought of *any* idiot getting their hands on Katelyn. Sweet Katelyn, who had never hurt a single spider or . . .

I shoved back to my feet, ignoring the twinge of pain in my knee.

"Get it together, Vik," I sang. "Get. It. Together."

The creak of the bathroom door brought me out of a livid spiral and back into the moment. Though Kate insisted she could drive home, neither Dahlia nor I thought it was a good idea. Her shift was over anyway, so I brought her back. Kate beelined for the shower and had been in there for the last fifteen minutes.

I sucked in a sharp breath and let it out in one long blow. The sound of her padding down the hall, toward her bedroom, bought me a few moments to get my coiled tension back under control.

I stood in the kitchen, gripped the counter, and closed my eyes.

Vini.

I needed Vini.

Time passed, but I wasn't sure how long. Too lost in my thoughts to make sense of it. Eventually, Katelyn's quiet voice startled the creeping edge of darkness that threatened to drown me.

"Vik?"

I straightened with a little smile. "Hey. Feel better?"

My heart knotted in my chest. Her wet hair lay on her shoulders, darker from the moisture. All evidence of makeup had been scrubbed off her face, but her eyes were still red and swollen from crying. I recalled the shape of her in my arms when she pressed herself into my chest and wanted to kill something all over again.

She managed a smile. "Yeah, thanks. I—"

"Don't apologize." I held up a hand, affecting a casual shrug. "We all have bad days."

Her face twisted, as if she were trying to decide something. Her mouth parted, lips frozen, before she finally nodded. Relief filled her features.

"Thanks."

More hung behind the word than the obvious. I reached for the handle to the microwave.

"Are you hungry?"

"Yeah, I think so."

"Dal? With yogurt afterward, of course."

She laughed a little. "Dal heals all wounds."

I almost winced, but acted as if I hadn't heard the lingering history in her words. The thinly-veiled pain. Kate's presence loosened the building fire inside me. At this rate, I'd at least make it through the next hour before exploding.

Relief replaced her uncertainty. She advanced farther into the room, dressed in a casual pair of leggings and an oversized shirt. No glasses interrupted her expression, leaving it clear as crystal.

"Can I help?"

I set her plate on the table. "Go for it, lady."

Her breath hitched slightly, and I realized too late that Appa's favorite nickname for Amma had just slipped out. To smooth the moment over, I rummaged through the fridge as if I hadn't said anything out of the normal.

In fact, I'd shocked myself.

Where the hell had that come from?

Deciding that the best path forward was the one where nothing had to be acknowledged tonight, I shut the fridge again. Containers cluttered my hands. Ten minutes later, she sat across from me at the table, a warmed bowl of dal in front of her. After a first taste of the spicy lentils, and a smile, she looked at me.

"It's delicious, as always."

"Amma would be so pleased, you think so." I gave her a warm smile that she reciprocated. "I need to head into physical therapy, but I'll be back in an hour or so. Are you all right?"

Her teeth sank into her bottom lip as she nodded. "Yes, thanks Vik. I really am sorry. I . . ."

"No explanation necessary until you're ready."

Tears pooled in her eyes, then disappeared as quickly. She smiled, head ducked a little as she picked up her spoon. A quiet, "Thanks," came next. With a few more exchanges, I slipped out the front door, internally seething.

Less than five minutes later, Vinita's voice filled my car. I turned a corner, navigating quietly out of the neighborhood.

"Hey, Vik."

"Tell me that Timothy Hanover didn't attack Katelyn five years ago. That he wasn't, for some *insane* reason, released back to the same town where he can stumble on her every day. I need to hear the words Vini, because I'm about to *lose* it."

Her astonished silence didn't make me feel any better.

"What? She told you?"

I pressed back against the seat and growled. "That's not what I wanted to hear."

"Explain, Vik," she snapped.

Slowly, I laid out the clues. What happened at the grocery store, and finally the text messages from Hernandez. Vini groaned.

"Poor Kate, I had no idea. Her story is not mine to tell, Vik. She's my best friend and I've been helping her through a few . . . tough times . . . with my colleague."

I ground my teeth together.

"That's confirmation, thanks."

"Vikram!" she cried. "Don't you dare do something stupid, like out her. She will tell you if and when she desires. You will act as if you know *nothing* and you will respect her privacy."

My breath was hot and fast.

"I won't just sit by and let her be afraid of this guy! He's out now, Vini. What if—"

"You aren't." Her firm tone knocked me off the shrinking ledge that felt too small. The anger I could barely keep under control. She softened. "You *are* helping her, Vik. She told me she feels safe with you, and she hasn't said that word for a long time. For heaven's sake, she's finally stopped talking about her rules! Let this play out, all right? You'll gain more trust if you let her come to you."

"I'm going to him first."

"You will not," she countered, huffy. "You will let Kinoshi secure the restraining order, and you will provide a safe place. The last thing she needs is drama. Believe it or not, Katelyn is not the emotionally abused girl that lives next door anymore. In five years and a lot of therapy, she's come a *long* way. Are there residuals? Absolutely, but she's working through them. Right now, she needs a friend and a safe place. You will be both."

Properly chastised, I closed my eyes.

"You're right."

"Of course I'm right."

"She's already put a restraining order together?"

"Yes. Kinoshi helped her with it after she received the call that he was getting out, probably on good behavior.."

Some of my ire calmed, but didn't drain away. It jumped around inside me like hot beans.

"Fine."

"Thunderstorms and darkness are her two biggest triggers. It . . . it happened when Timothy was high on meth and drunk."

"At Trina's house, I presume?"

"The rest is hers to tell." Tears pooled in her voice, making it husky and deep. "Vik, please, take care of her. Keep her safe, okay? That girl means more to me than any sister ever could have. The last five years have been really hard on her. Promise?"

"I will," I whispered. "I promise to protect her."

The words rang in my head for a long time after I hung up the phone. By the time I returned home from physical therapy, my thoughts had straightened out. All murderous intent had been set aside for now.

Like it or not, *everything* had changed. My focus turned to Katelyn, though I wanted to pummel Timothy into the earth until he resembled dust more than a man. She wouldn't have to live in fear with me. No more hiding. No more cowering. It was time to remind her how to *live* again. If I knew anything, it was how to press life to its utmost limits.

Now she could, too.

Because I would always protect her.

* * *

"Oh."

The breathy word escaped Kate a week later. She climbed out of my Jeep and stared out, wide-eyed. A wall of trees ringed a haphazard parking lot. Little more than trampled grass and a half-mile two-track road had led here from the highway. She blinked, breath arrested, then shot her incredulous gaze to mine.

I grinned.

"Tempest Lake."

Brightness blazed across her features in a dazzling smile. "Really? I haven't been here in years."

"I figured."

My car door closed as I cut off annoyed thoughts about how small she'd been living her life, all because of an idiot that couldn't control himself. A backpack waited in the trunk, brimming with snacks, water bottles, and a few towels. Kate stepped away from the car, clad in a pair of tight jeans shorts that made my mouth water, and a pair of hiking sandals that protected her toes.

I slung the backpack over my shoulder.

"Let's go."

Wordless, she wandered in my wake.

A footpath cut through knee-high grasses, similar to an animal trail. This particular lake—more sprawling pond than anything—was a local hangout. Tourists didn't know to explore this windy part of the dirt roads, and private land on either side shielded it from use. Daniel owned the land where we parked and made sure that locals didn't spread the word about it.

Amma, Appa, Vini, Kate, and I came here often as children.

The gentle song of birds, and a patter of leaves overhead, escorted us deeper into the forest. I breathed deeply the scent of warm grass and loamy earth, and my stride began to meander. I slowed when Kate made a delighted noise in her throat. She crouched over a bright blue wildflower, bobbing on a tall stalk. It faced her, as if smiling at a new source of sunshine.

She beamed back.

The tip of her finger touched the silky petal before she straightened and began to walk again. Never in my life had I felt so jealous of a flower. A second later, a similar squeal issued. I twisted to find her unearthing half a bird's nest near a tree root, just off the trail. Concern filled her gaze as she canted her eyes overhead. I laughed, reading her thoughts.

"The birds are fine," I said. "That's from last year. See the way the twigs are weathered? It's old. The mama bird kicked it out and started fresh."

Clearly relieved, she tucked the nest into a fold of bark, and we kept going.

Similar treasures found Katelyn. Half of the shell of a bright blue robin's egg, empty and speckled with darker tones. Grasses braided together. A tree that grew into a c-shape before jutting back up to the same angle as before.

"You're an enjoy-as-you-walk kind of person, then?" I asked in a musing tone as she studied a cairn of rocks set off to the side, marking another trail that led to the farther side of the lake. I waited in the middle of the footpath, head canted back to study an oak tree.

She grinned, unabashed. "What's the point of the forest," she murmured, "if you don't really see it? Oooh! There are magenta flowers up here?"

I stared at her profile, illuminated by the trees surrounding her with long arms, and silently agreed.

We meandered a few feet per minute. Kate exclaimed over a dozen different flowers, a couple weeds, the thickness of trees in one part, the open meadow in another. She collected flower colors like a child and giggled next to me when I teased her about her slow pace.

For my purpose? We went just fast enough.

Sunshine freckled the ground in spots, and warm rays alternately danced across her skin, illuminating an already radiant expression.

I soaked her up.

Thirty minutes later, we emerged out of the tunnel of trees and onto the muddy bank of Tempest Lake. I stopped, sucking in a sharp breath. All these years that I'd stayed near Pineville after my parents moved away, and I hadn't visited here, a place that meant so much.

What had I been doing with my life?

Right. Chasing women. Empty hours. Trying to forget something I didn't want to unearth again. Trying to remember who I thought I should be, instead of who I wanted to be. Such a life felt dumber every day.

Kate squealed.

"Vik! It's exactly the same."

A hushed reverence bore her forward. She climbed onto a black, moss-strewn boulder and stood on top. A picture of her and Vinita at eleven-years-old at that exact spot, clasped in each other's skinny arms, stood on my parents' dresser at home, right next to Amma's statue of Lord Ganesha. Kate held out her arms and spun.

"It hasn't changed," she cried.

"Amazing, isn't it?"

The cut of the shoreline against the trees, the gentle slope of land to mud, reeds, then water, looked exactly the way I remembered it. Sunlight glinted off the top, glimmering in white sparkles. Pearlescent clouds chugged by overhead, reflected in the crystal-clear mountain water, as azure as the sky.

Kate lowered and sat on the warm boulder, legs dangling off. Her tanned thighs beckoned me, but I kept my gaze deferred.

"Let's go swimming," she said quickly. "We have to! For old times sake. I don't have any extra clothes, but . . ."

Laughing, I dropped the backpack. "I'm glad you suggested it, because I am ready for such a thing. Hope you don't mind, but I grabbed some of your shorts and a tank before we left. I couldn't find a swimming suit."

Color brushed her cheeks. "I don't have one."

Shock dropped my jaw.

"You don't?"

Her gaze skated away with a half-shrug that was more uncertainty than defensiveness. "I haven't gone swimming in . . . a long time."

Many things about Kate surprised me these days, but this felt like a shock of lightning. Kate and water had always made sense. It had been her happy place. Amma and Appa had a hard time keeping her out of it. She took to water like a fish. I used to call her guppy.

"Why not?"

She swallowed. "I guess it just . . . it didn't seem that safe."

Those words fell between us like a miasma. My hands tightened on my backpack before I brushed all of this aside. The past was in the past—couldn't change that now. But dammit, we were swimming today and we'd do it every day if she wanted to.

"Well," I said with forced cheer, "I wanted to surprise you with this, so I brought some spares. You can swim in clothes as easily as a swimming suit."

Instead of annoyance, her eyes sparkled back in delight.

"Yes!"

I tossed the backpack at her feet to rummage through, then slipped my shirt off, kicking my shoes to the side. Already prepared, I had my swim trunks on. The water would be warm and luxurious at this part of the summer. I waded in until it covered my ankles. The loose mud at the bottom squelched between my toes, thick and soft. It distracted my thoughts while Kate slinked away to change in privacy.

Memories filtered through my mind, free to wander like the clouds. Amma unloading a picnic on a wide blanket. Appa attempting to fish, muttering swear words under his breath that earned chastisements from Amma. Vini and Kate chasing bugs and frogs along the shore. I'd brought several girlfriends here—the rock made an excellent make-out spot—but all of those felt vacant in the glow of family memories.

Or maybe it was Kate.

Next to her, everything felt like a hollowed-out shell.

A flash of color streaked by my right side, then ended in a squeal and a hearty splash. Astonished, I registered that Kate had run past me and thrown herself into the water, cannon-ball style, seconds after the water splashed my cheeks. She stood, cackling hysterically, and my throat tightened.

Quiet, mousy Kate wore a pair of athletic shorts and a sports bra. Her hair cluttered around her face, wet and tousled.

So much lovely skin.

Heart hammering, I shuffled into the water, grateful for the hidden escape my aviators provided. Damn, but I hadn't thought this out. Alone with Kate, who sparkled like a star, with so much of her body I'd want to touch.

Nope, I commanded myself. *Get it back together.*

She dropped back into the water, taking to it like a fish. With a gleeful sound, she swam deeper. It dropped off not far from this gentle entrance, and soon she tread water. Nothing but green trees and blue skies joined us. Shallow waters gave way to cooler depths as the muddy bottom disappeared, but the chill refreshed against a bold sun.

"Hey, guppy," I called. "Wait for the slow poke."

Kate laughed and slicked hair out of her eyes. "I loved swimming in the lake with Vini and Appa."

I really laughed then. "Appa and his hairy chest. The man could swim forever with so much hair making him buoyant."

She giggled, and the shared memory warmed me as much as the sunshine. I leaned back, letting the summer heat tilt across my neck.

"Thanks, Vik." Her smile stretched so far her eyes crinkled. "I'd forgotten about this place. It makes me feel like your parents are here, and we're kids again. We made so many great memories."

"Like the time Vini tried to jump from a tree into the water and broke her ankle?"

She laughed. "You had to carry her out on your back."

"She screamed in my ear the whole time," I muttered.

"Or Appa forgot to pack up the food, and a bear came in the night. Amma was so angry." Another peal of laughter joined the first. "She never let him live it down."

"Vini slept through Amma shrieking when the bear nosed her tent." I snorted. "She always slept like the dead."

Kate twirled through the water, like a sprite brought back to life. With neat wake lines soaring out from either side, she cut across the lake, toward a fallen tree. Moss dotted the water-darkened top.

I followed like a helpless puppy.

The morning passed in a quiet lake adventure, without another soul to be seen except Kate. She drew tiny miracles to her. Speckles of moss that floated on top in the shape of a dragon. Peeping baby birds in a nest. A quiet fawn on the far side of the lake that didn't startle when Kate watched it, curious as a kitten.

She quietly grabbed my arm and pressed a finger to her lips. Not far away, a dragonfly hovered over the water, then sped off. The far reach of Tempest Lake drew a mother moose and her calf in, then back into the weeds after they drank. Nature warbled lazily around us, quiet, messy, and calm. A new side of Kate—an open, unafraid side—sprawled with glittering array.

Vini had been right.

Adulthood had ushered her into the world a totally different, stronger version of herself. I couldn't help my rapture over such a transformation. The urge to form a glass bubble around us, keep us in this moment forever, crept over me as the minutes ticked by.

Hours later, she sat cross-legged on a blanket. Her shirt was damp where her wet bra touched it, her hair loose and drying around her ears. She popped a grape into her mouth and peered into the trees thoughtfully.

"It's been so long," she murmured.

I sprawled next to her on my side, toying with a piece of long-stemmed grass. Seeds gathered on the ends, jingling together. "Since what?"

"Since . . . nothing."

"Nothing?"

"I haven't just done *nothing* in awhile. Not in a way that felt so . . ."

"Safe?"

Her brow cocked, then she nodded. I hadn't meant to supply the word, but couldn't stop it once it was out. For Kate, the word had to feel loaded, fragile. The utter peace of her expression gave her away.

"I'm glad," I said softly.

A touch landed on my shoulder. Startled, I tilted my head back to see her peering at me with a half-smile.

"Thank you."

Unable to speak, I just nodded. She lay back, legs long, and stacked her hands behind her head. Like a cat in sunshine, she sprawled out, arms golden in the summer sun. The urge to throw my arm around her ribs, pull her close, and nuzzle into her neck swept over me. I tucked the grass in between my teeth and stared at the water instead.

A brewing truth stirred. I didn't fight it, but I wouldn't look directly at it either. I'd never felt it before and I needed to weigh it out, inspect it, figure out what it wanted.

Dredges of my previous relationships—one could scoff at the word, because I'd never truly really committed to many—arose from the depths of mind and soul. Arms-length had been simple enough. Lonely, but easy.

Remembrances slipped out from their hiding places around Kate, and this enchanting moment was no different. She was too much light and goodness in one space to let the darkness stay, like holding a moonbeam.

Transcendent, but slippery.

Such retrospections returned now, ushered by a shuddering realization that all my life, I'd intentionally played with something that wasn't . . . real. Passion. Infatuation. Amma's lectures to find a woman with a good family and make babies bounced around my head. Now, they settled for the first time.

Who wants someone else forever? I used to think.

Now, I wondered if maybe forever wasn't long enough.

Kate stirred up passion and infatuation for me in spades, yet it didn't stop there. Unlike all the others, the tendrils of her power unfurled far longer, far deeper, than anyone else had gone before. Roots digging into the unbroken, dry, cracked surface of my heart.

Why?

The answers eluded me. In the midst of such thoughts, only one thing seemed abundantly clear.

Damn, but I'd fallen hard.

Chapter Thirteen

KATELYN

"So," Vini drawled. "You went to Tempest Lake last week?"

A warm wash of recollection flowed through me after her inquiring tone, though the lingering note set me on edge. Vini fished for something when she elongated her vowels like that. I smiled just to set her off. Her probing gaze studied me through the phone, her lovely face framed in a cut bob of black hair, tapered back.

"It was so fun."

"The pictures looked like it."

"We stayed for four or five hours."

"You didn't camp?"

"Not this time."

I set aside a shirt I'd folded to hang it up later, and reached for a pair of pants. Vikram was at work, leaving me alone in the house with chores and oddities for the day. A pair of panties hung off a peg near the back window to dry, next to one of my favorite bras. Littered amongst stuff in the kitchen was a half-eaten package of my favorite crackers, a mug of tea from breakfast, and a note for Vikram to call Amma in my handwriting.

Amidst the same gentle mess lingered Vikram. A tube of his

favorite honey lip balm. A business card for a new yoga studio on the other side of town, and a hastily-scratched card with a Senegalese recipe for chicken yassa. We both lived in a not-messy-but-not-neat in-between, with the stuff of life spilling out the edges.

Like . . . home.

Without Vini, the only home I would have ever known was decorated with used syringes, littered bodies, and crushed beer cans. Yet another way her family saved me.

Vini sighed. "Tempest Lake sounds like a dream. I haven't been there in ten years, and I miss it. Except for that one time I broke my ankle and Vikram bellyached about carrying me back. Remember?"

I giggled. "Definitely. How's the baby?"

Vini blew a raspberry, then held the phone out to show her burgeoning baby belly. I squealed, unable to help it. She panned back to her face. "I'm showing now, which is fun, but I'm already ready for this to be over."

My lips pulled into a compassionate grimace. "Wish I was there to give you a foot massage."

"Me too!" she cried, then laughed. "Zayne just isn't the same. Speaking of Zayne, talk to me about what it's like to live with adult Vik. Is he totally annoying like teenager Vik? Does he clean up after himself, or is he super messy?"

My head tilted to the side. I paused, mid-reach for another pair of pants to fold. "What does Vikram have to do with Zayne?"

"Nothing," she said sharply, but with amusement, "but I think you're hiding something about my brother from me and I have to know what it is!"

"Vini, if something happened, you would be the first to know."

"Would I?"

Her challenging tone caught me. Would I tell her if Vik

made a move? Unlikely, at least at first. I glanced up. Vini's eyes widened.

"He's not there, is he?"

"No, he's doing an orientation thing for a new job at the Outfitters. He starts next week, on the two-month anniversary of his surgery."

Her nose wrinkled. "Well, that's good. I'm glad he has a purpose in life. Now, stop ducking my question. Has anything happened?" She gasped. "Has he kissed you?"

I choked and tossed a pair of socks into a pile on top of the dryer.

"Kissed me?"

Her mouth popped open, "Did he?"

"No! You're the worst. Nothing is happening. We're friends."

"Hmm."

"He took me to Tempest Lake and it was . . . fun. That's it, Vini."

"But you love him."

An aggravated sigh escaped me. I should never have told her. I batted that aside, as if it didn't change everything.

"Last night, we sat on the couch and watched a monster movie again. It was terrible and wonderful at the same time. He loves to cook, I love to eat, and we see each other in between shifts. It's . . . kind of boring, honestly."

A bald-faced lie. Living with Vikram was like constantly touching lightning. Electrifying. Every moment laden with a whisper of *what if*. A near-touch in the kitchen. His enigmatic smile lit up the room. I'd fallen asleep on the couch two days ago and woke up to the smell of him wrapped around me. He'd covered me with a blanket, then left a light on after going to bed.

Vini pulled me back to consciousness with her skeptical throat-noise.

"Mm hmm."

"There's nothing!" I cried, though I felt transparently in denial. "It's just . . . wonderful and easy and living with Vik is like living with you. It's natural."

Vinita's gaze tapered to slashes. "You sound an awful lot like you're trying to convince yourself of something."

Despite myself, I laughed softly. "I am," I admitted. The sundress in my hands dropped back to the dryer as I leaned my elbows on top and put my head in my hands. "Oh, Vini. I'm in so much trouble."

"Why?"

"Because . . . I'm so deeply in love with him."

The words choked in my throat, but I couldn't take them back. Wouldn't, even if I complained about Vini bugging me too much. How could I hide anything from her, anyway? She knew the intricacies of the mapped portions of my heart and soul. It had been a pointless attempt to play what we had off as nothing.

A giggle escaped her. "Amma would die if you and Vik ended up together. Die of ultimate joy. I haven't said a word to her because she'd press him and henpeck him into it, but know that we are both on your side."

My face crumpled. I shook my head. "Vini, c'mon. He's Vik. The man has kissed more women—and who knows what else he's done with them—than I could even fathom. He spent years of his life dodging relationships for a reason. Just because he hasn't been dating the past six or seven months doesn't mean that part of him is gone."

"True," she murmured, "but Vik has ghosts too, you know."

I paused, straightening. My phone was propped against the detergent, revealing my startled expression.

"What do you mean?"

"Don't you remember Emma?"

Emma. I wracked my memories, combing through them. A niggling of familiarity came with the name, but nothing obvious at first.

"Emma?"

Vini nodded. "It's not my story to tell," she murmured in the calm way that she did, but hinted at deeper intricacies, "but he had his heart broken before. Sort of curled into himself after that, then kept everyone at arm's distance. Happened in high school and spurred this huge drama my parents had to get involved with. The Merry Idiots really saved him, in some ways. Grady had detention over it—this whole mess."

"How do I *not* remember this?"

A portion of Vik's timeline hadn't been opened to me? That didn't feel right at all.

"Vik was a playboy for a reason. Because of this foundational thing with Emma, he's never trusted women. I wrote a paper on him in college, but changed the name to someone else. He never found out."

She giggled to herself.

The dark side of my shining Indian god knocked some of the air out of my sails, but no love from my heart. Whatever he faced, I'd willingly brave it with him.

Wouldn't I?

I swallowed. Yes. Whole-heartedly, but that didn't mean I could trust it. Not yet. Not until I knew and understood more.

"Can Vik actually settle down into a relationship with one person for more than three weeks? That's the question I'm turning over in my mind," I asked, relieved to have someone I could ask.

"He's never invited anyone else to live with him."

"Yeah, but he probably sees me like a sister."

She made a dismissive noise. "Stop that, you know it's not entirely true. Yes, he cares for you. Yes, you're part of the family. Does that mean his feelings have remained entirely platonic? Not by a long shot."

A flutter of hope lit me up inside. "Really?"

Vini laughed, and the phone shook as she straightened it. "Yes! Really. Don't you see it?"

"I want to."

"Then look for it."

"What if it's all in my head and I make it up out of desperation and it's not real?"

"You wouldn't do that."

"How do *you* know?"

"You're a brave and ferocious woman, Kate. No one has strength like you. Time to pull on your big girl panties and face the truth, all right? Vik is a safe spot for you in more ways than one, and that's all I'm going to say."

The words sank into me, like my toes in the murky bottom of Tempest Lake. Oh, if they were true . . . Barely able to catch the thought, I let it flutter away, lost in the morass of my mind.

"Thanks."

"Talk to me about Timothy." She straightened, all business now. "Is the restraining order in place yet? Have you seen him? What news on that front?"

Startled, I leaned back. "I haven't heard from Kinoshi once I dropped it off, and he said he'd let me know."

Vini smiled. "Good. Now you can focus on more important things, like when you're going to marry my brother. So you haven't seen Timothy again?"

"Just that time at the grocery store that I told you about," I murmured, thoughtful now.

My mind wandered over the last week. Since Tempest Lake, I'd been in a sort of summery, happy daze. Hours at work flew by, and the time at home with Vik wasn't long enough. A low-level thrum of euphoria glazed each hour together, even the boring ones. Though we had no formal agreement, and touches were frequent and fleeting, his attention and laughter brightened every aspect of my life.

Yet when had I let Timothy glide into the background?

Somewhere in the safe shuffle of living, kept away from the ills of the world by Vik's home.

His very presence.

"Well, I need to go," Vini said with a sigh. "I have an online appointment coming up in ten minutes. Just wanted to hear about Tempest Lake and make sure you weren't still living in denial over how you feel about my brother."

"I've never denied how much I loved him."

"True. But now you're protecting yourself and, in this case, it may not be needed. You're denying *him* loving you, and that's the same thing."

A smile slipped across my lips. "Thanks, Vini. I'll keep you updated. Love you. Kiss the baby for me."

With a smile, she ended the video call. I turned back to the rest of my laundry, piled at the bottom of the dryer. One of Vikram's shirts that I'd thrown into the washer with mine tangled into a pair of pants. Both came out next. I stopped, lifted the shirt to my nose, and drew in a deep breath.

Sunshine.

Leaves.

Wild things.

A thought occurred to me with stunning clarity: I hadn't reviewed my rules in days.

* * *

A manilla folder landed on the desk in front of me, pages fluttering like bird wings under the heavier shell. My name was written across the top in neat, black lines. Kinoshi smiled.

"Your restraining order is filed."

"Really?"

"All done. You now hold a restraining order against Timothy Hanover."

Relief tripled through me. "That's . . . a huge burden off of me, Kinoshi. Thank you for acting so quickly."

He frowned. "I would have liked to see it done faster, but there's no pushing the courts. It's through now, so you have some legal recourse against him should he attempt anything. Perhaps not tangible protection, but it's something."

"Better than nothing."

Kinoshi tilted his head. "Yes. Preparation, for sure. We'll be able to act more decisively should he violate parole. I've seen him once or twice around Pineville now. Have you?"

I nodded.

Compassion filled his gaze. "Did he see you?"

"Once that I know of."

"Are you handling this change all right? It must feel invasive to have him near your hometown, where you were once safe."

His concern startled me. Kinoshi had been more kind than I expected from such a professional attorney, with sincere compassion for his clients. Never had I once felt afraid with him, and that meant so much.

Answering his question was more difficult than I expected. The safety Vikram provided had created a buffer against Timothy's return to my life. Now, I wasn't sure how I truly felt about the situation.

Everything else was so . . . nebulous.

The world felt distant with Vikram close and safety tangible. The slipping of my rules made me feel like nothing was concrete anymore, and I couldn't form an opinion either way.

"I think I'm handling it all right?" I shrugged. "Honestly, I'm . . . not sure."

Kinoshi leaned forward, a pen in his hands that he tapped on a pad of paper. "With any luck, once this is delivered to Timothy as well, he'll get tired of trying to avoid you and just move away. If either of you leave, it should be him, not you. It's a small town. He owes it to you."

A hesitant smile followed. "Thanks. Seems like too much to ask for."

"I have . . ." he paused, as if deciding something. A little shake of his head came next. "I thought I heard word that he might be . . . spoken of in not-so-great circles around here and Jackson City. There's a possibility he's making trouble. A few rumors of drugs, maybe some stealing. It's all through other cases and idle gossip in town. I work frequently with the county officers and sometimes get updates. People have reported seeing him near their garages at night after clear evidence of tampering, a few other things. Just . . . be careful?"

My gut clenched.

"Of course."

Kinoshi held up two hands. "It may be nothing and there's no proof against him, but getting out of prison is a desperate thing. It's not an easy world to come out of, and we don't have a lot of programs to assist people back to productive lives in the community. I've seen released inmates wallow in real life and eventually return to prison for good. While we never want that, we also don't want your safety to be compromised. At the hearing, Timothy struck me as a bitter man who didn't see his own guilt. I'd hate for that to come back on you."

The reminder cooled some of my newfound gusto for life, but I appreciated the grounding. My happy life with Vikram had lulled me into a more secure place. One where I didn't need so many rules, where my safety wasn't solely my own concern. For the first time in weeks, I questioned whether any of that was real.

With Timothy at large, I had no way of knowing what he'd do in a desperate situation. Vikram couldn't stay near me forever. Eventually, I'd have to protect myself.

But that time wasn't yet.

I pulled myself out of the instant floundering with a little breath.

Kinoshi nodded to the folder. "Take it and stay in touch. I'm here if you ever need anything, all right?"

He stood, and I followed suit. "Thanks, Kinoshi."

"Anytime."

Sunshine warmed my shoulders as I stepped out of his office and headed down the street. Kinoshi wasn't far from the Frolicking Moose, where my shift would start any moment now. The brief walk down the road gave my thoughts a chance to settle. I hugged the folder close to my chest and tried not to be too conspicuous as I surveyed the street.

The burning question wouldn't be ignored, however.

When should I tell Vik?

When I arrived, Dahlia and Bastian sat together in his usual booth. He kept an arm curled protectively around her waist as he nodded to me.

"Shop is all yours!" Dahlia cried, with a bright smile. She tossed me her apron, which I caught. "Bastian is taking me on a date."

"Go have fun, lovebirds."

Leslie stood behind the counter, fulfilling a to-go order that pulled into the drive-thru. She waved as I set the folder on Leslie's work table, grabbed an apron, and tied it around my waist. Customers shuffled into the store. I greeted them and stepped behind the counter, grateful to fall into familiar routines while my thoughts whirled around Timothy.

The hours eased by in small talk with Leslie. Her youngest son stopped in, and they took off to go shopping in Jackson City, leaving the shop to me. My conversation with Kinoshi left me on edge. Though I tried to loosen up, I couldn't stop surveying the street every ten seconds.

"I'm safe," I murmured, thumb to my palm. "I'm safe."

Despite no evidence to the contrary, Kinoshi's warning looped through my mind like a newsreel.

A few rumors of drugs. A bitter man who didn't see his own guilt. The words conjured memories of the trial. Short, yet awful. My disbelief over Timothy's surprise couldn't be denied, though the rape kit made reality irrefutable. I grabbed the folder, gazing over the restraining order in a quiet moment. When another customer stepped inside, I set the folder down and attempted to stuff the implications away for later.

Not ever, if I could help it.

A few minutes later, a jingle on the door caught my attention. My head snapped up, breath caught, until my gaze landed on a jaw sharp enough to cut rock and a charming grin. Vikram pulled the aviators off his eyes. A white shirt stretched over thick shoulders and made my stomach catch.

He stepped closer, tousled hair tied hastily out of his face.

"Hey, lady."

Every movement drew my attention closer to him. The way his hair shone, his lips twitched, a hint of stubble darkened his cheeks. With Vikram near, the enclosing panic ebbed away. I breathed easier, which I appreciated and hated at the same time. How could he affect me so deeply?

His luminous expression sobered.

"You all right, Kate?"

I forced a smile. "Yes, better now."

My heart gave a little skip. Had that been too forward? Revealed too much? With a quick glance at the shop, he slipped around the counter and pulled me into his arms.

"You look like you could use a hug."

I sighed, cheek pressed to his chest. His touchy nature and instinctive compassion worked against me. I had no reason to assume Vikram meant anything but support from the gesture, but I wanted it to be so different.

"Thanks."

He pulled away. His fingers lingered for a second on my side, then disappeared. I longed to pull them back, then ask if I could stay forever.

"Just wanted to stop by after my first shift," he said. Amusement quirked his lips a little higher at the edges, as if he saw something funny. "I have physical therapy and needed to burn some time before it starts."

"I'm glad you did. How was the first day?"

He shrugged. "Uneventful. Difficult to hold myself back from buying gear. Daniel makes it easy and I've run a register before. Shouldn't be a problem. It's nice to be back in the world again." A shudder slipped through him. "I was starting to hate my couch."

I laughed, grateful for the reprieve from my own mind. "Green tea?"

"Please."

The bell rang, indicating a drive-through order. With a look, I commanded him not to move and back-stepped away. He held up both hands in promise and leaned against the counter to wait.

By the time I finished scurrying around for croissants, cake pops, a macchiato, and a cappuccino to go, Vik had turned around. His arms braced against the countertop. My heart did a double-slam in my chest. Vik stared down at the folder from Kinoshi's, my name scrawled across the top.

Propelled by white-hot terror, I slipped to his side, grabbed his shoulder, and whirled him around. He spun right into my arms and our lips met in a kiss.

I melted.

Then I panicked.

Before I could pull away, his shock had already faded. He reached up, put a hand on my cheek, and pulled me closer. Any thoughts of departure fled—he held me too tight. His sturdy palm against the hollow of my cheek melted me. I leaned into him, limp. My heart turned into a storm. My breath dropped out the bottom. All I knew was his beckoning siren call.

The languid pull of his body against mine.

Vik warmed into the kiss in a hot second, intensifying it

moments later. He razed my soul. Plundered years of adoration with a single kiss. All fears fractured and all thoughts fled except for one.

Kissing.

Vikram.

He pulled away just a breath, but didn't release me. Our lips could graze each other, a thin layer from returning.

My body stiffened as I waited for judgment or comment or . . .

The drive-though bell pealed through the air.

Awkward now, I cleared my throat. When I took a step back, the room spun. I reached for the counter to stabilize. He lowered his hands to my shoulders. He held me firm. Immovable. An unreadable expression filled his face when he murmured, "Kate?"

The low question brought me firmly back to reality. Was he asking what that meant? Did he have a question or was it all just hypothetical and surreal at this point as well?

My voice squeaked when I cried, "Gotta get that!"

Like a coward, I retreated to the window. The order kept me inordinately focused away from him, though I felt as if I saw nothing *but* him. He stood in the same spot, all languor and grace, as I struggled to make the till work.

Something smiled down on me, because a second car slipped through next. I attended to it, hands still shaky. By the time I finished their order, I had pulled myself back together.

This is fine, I told myself. *I have time to tell him the truth when I'm ready. It's mine to own, not his. We have no obligation to each other.*

It was just a kiss.

Yet, a fractured part of my heart quivered anyway.

I drew in a deep breath, closed the window, and spun around to face him.

Vikram was gone.

Chapter Fourteen

VIKRAM

Idiot.

Idiot.

Idiot.

The word banged through my head with each step that carried me away from the Frolicking Moose, closer to my car, closer to freedom. To air. To the ability to think and breathe at the same time.

Insufferable heat billowed free when I opened the door and ducked inside, but I ignored it. Sweat beaded on my forehead when I cranked the car on, slung my seatbelt across my chest, and peeled out of the parking lot. Right about now, Katelyn might be noticing that I was the biggest. wimp. ever.

Why had I run?

Stupid question. I knew *exactly* why I slipped the hell out of there. A storm of emotion bubbled in my chest with an underlying ferocity. It tightened my lungs. Crashed my heart. Wreaked havoc on a spot I once held in greatest locked protection. No more. Kate had effectively smashed everything that once held me together.

Every guard.

Every prison.

Self-imposed jail may not sound like a very fun time, but control sure felt better than *this* wild, slippery ride of emotion. A slide of destruction and devastation that only love could create.

Only when Pineville existed in my rearview mirror, and the open highway sprawled like a gray artery in front of me, did I begin to fully breathe again. The heat of Kate's kiss lingered on my lips like a burn. It sparked, like life essence, all the way through to my fingertips. There was no halt to the power. She'd already crashed into me. The pieces were too small to glue into the same Vikram again.

With a growl, I pulled off at a random point on the highway, parked away from cars whizzing past. I shoved my hands through my hair.

"Get. It. Together."

It all happened so quickly.

One moment I pretended like I didn't see her restraining order paperwork, and the next one I whipped around and into her arms. Did she kiss me as a distraction?

Maybe.

But then it became something else entirely.

Her lips had been just as eager as mine, as quick to respond. Her sexy gasp of surprise had only heightened the moment. I closed my eyes, scrubbed my hand over my face. My heart continued to slam in protest, so hard it rocked my chest. The percussive beats shoved blood all the way to my toes.

I tilted my head back.

Space gave me too much room to think now, and regret followed. Not for kissing her—or did she kiss me? No one could regret a chemistry so thick. Regret for running chased me now. For not knowing what to do or say. I'd kissed-and-run with countless women before. Laughed about romanticized ideas around affection and closeness.

The universe mocked me.

Minutes passed. Maybe hours. The world continued on around my oblivious, frightened bubble. At the heart of this lay one sordid, nasty, buried-too-deep-to-see-it-clearly truth.

I had felt this way before.

This bubbling, happy anxiety. The thrill of a chase, of a connection. A feeling buried deep in a pit I'd long tried to ignore. Kate wasn't the first woman to affect me this deeply.

No, Emma Goldmann held that accolade.

The honor went to a seventeen-something-year-old-girl that, in one fell swoop, taught me the ways of the world. Taught me who *not* to be if I didn't want to experience crushing regret or harrowing sorrow.

Emma.

A woman I hadn't thought of in fifteen years. Or maybe I thought about her all the time, but wouldn't acknowledge it. She hovered on the surface of everything, and nothing, at the same time.

"Kate isn't Emma, you idiot," I muttered.

Didn't work.

Reality would never erase wounds like this.

The echo of Emma's name rang in my soul as I turned my car back to life. No reason to go back into ancient history. No good came from dredging up the past, opening old wounds, bleeding historical scars. Not even the big ones.

The ugly ones.

The engine chugged, started, and settled. Air conditioning caressed my face again as I turned my thoughts back to life. If I raced, I'd make it to my physical therapy appointment on time. Life needed to happen. Something *except* thinking about her body smashed against mine, only not out of fear or panic.

I had to fix this.

Somehow.

* * *

My keys clattered when they landed on a hook suspended from the wall near my door. The townhouse lay quiet, even though Kate's car was parked outside. No lights. No stirrings. I locked the door behind me.

Carefully, I stole my way down the hall and toward her bedroom. The door lay canted open an inch. Before I peered inside, I gently rapped on the door with my knuckles. My knee ached from physical therapy, and my stomach growled with hunger. I'd been distracted the whole session, thinking about what an idiot I'd been.

No sound came from inside.

I peeked inside to see her curled in a ball on the bed, eyes closed. Her breaths expanded and dropped in regular, wispy intervals. I paused, then leaned my head against her doorframe. I didn't have it in me to wake her up. All the things I'd collected in my head to say dropped.

Somehow, I needed to let her know that she wasn't like the others. That I thought I was ready for something different in a way I never had been before, though I couldn't put my finger on why or how.

Could I actually commit to someone?

I never had before, not truly. The deep knowing in my chest told me yes, I could do this. Would Kate believe me, though? Her skepticism couldn't be blamed.

It meant something to me, I wanted to say.

Instead, I stole away, the ghost of her kiss heady in my mind.

Chapter Fifteen

KATELYN

The next day, I grumped around the Frolicking Moose in a bad attempt not to reveal how stirred-up that kiss made me.

That accident.

Could kisses be an accident? Or had my subconscious finally taken over and drawn us together in an explicitly defiant way?

Regardless of the reason, it happened. No going back now.

Had to face this hurricane.

A pair of subdued black-rimmed glasses pulled my hair away from my face, out of my eyes. I'd shoved them behind my ears the moment I woke, ready to screen myself from the world. Vikram's retreat to his bedroom for the night certainly hadn't helped my state of mind. I'd hidden from him, too.

The thought that I may have just ruined everything haunted me all night long, escorting the compulsive urge to hide behind my glasses to the forefront. All my courage had nearly dissipated when I stumbled into the bathroom this morning. Vik's bedroom door lay open, the bed made. No sign of him lingered in the house, except for a red heart written in dry-erase marker on the mirror.

It sent my chest fluttering almost as much as our kiss.

What did that mean? Something, certainly. I'd just convinced myself into the idea that Vik would kick me out, ask me to leave, when he forced me to consider an alternative.

Maybe he *liked* the kiss.

Vikram had always been a relentless flirt, but he hadn't always put forward something that could be construed. With Vini's reassurances still in my head after our conversation, I clung to the hope that his gesture in marker meant more than my brain downplayed.

Yet, I didn't have the courage to text him about it. This conversation needed to happen face-to-face. No matter how much I feared it.

Leslie bustled in and out of her office in the hallway all morning, pulling down summer decorations, putting up new ones. Pinning a banner about wildfires to a community board and removing business cards. The methodical movements of the day allowed me to think more clearly.

"Gotta grab a few things in Jackson for the HomeBnb restock." Leslie drummed her fingernails on the counter as she swept by. "You okay to manage by yourself?"

"Yep. Got it."

"See you in a few hours!"

Sunshine glinted off her blonde hair as she stepped outside, purse tucked under her arm. No customers lingered while I scrubbed down a few machines, so I sank further into the quiet with gratitude.

A happy shout rang outside. I peered out the drive-through window to see a few kids scamper by, where the lake lingered not far from the shop. A lightly pebbled beach gave way to murky mud and trees here and there. A family strode by, headed to the rivers that converted into the body of water.

Behind them, lurked a figure.

In the water, up to his ankles, stood Timothy.

My chest seized. I ducked out of sight with a sharp breath, my stomach dropping to my ankles. Then I peered back out from the very edge of the window with one eye. Timothy didn't seem to have noticed me.

In fact, he didn't seem to be doing . . . much.

He wore baggy jeans, a beat up pair of shoes, and a ratty old t-shirt. Dirt caked most of his clothes, as if he hadn't washed them in awhile. The sun bore down on him as he stared out at the water. Several brown bags lay at his feet. Alcohol bottles inside, perhaps? Based on the vague packaging, I couldn't be sure.

Tucked away where he didn't see me watching, I took advantage of the moment to adjust to this new reality. I remained back, out of sight. Did he know that I worked here? Where did he live now? The questions populated endlessly as I stared at him, sick to my stomach. If he was drunk . . .

Five years ago, I'd been a vulnerable, young girl. The ways of violent men and drug cartels weren't new to me—my aunt had introduced me to that way of life very quickly after my mother died—but Timothy had been something I didn't expect. In a flash, he'd taken what felt like everything.

Yet, it wasn't.

Years of therapy reminded me of core truths. I wasn't defined by the actions of others. He didn't change my value with his drug-addled, violent assault. Timothy would wallow for the rest of his life in terrible decisions and bad situations and I would choose something better.

But it didn't stop the memories.

Recalling the night was inevitable; I knew this day could happen. While Timothy stared, unmoving at the edge of the lake, I didn't look away. I *made* myself see him. Acknowledge his existence in this world. A fact that, until now, I tried to pretend didn't exist.

The ability to see him while remaining hidden was an uncanny gift. A chance to process and step forward, but without the pressure of his rage-hardened eyes.

Still . . . memories.

Overwhelmed now, I stepped further away from the edge of the window. If he looked over his shoulder, he wouldn't be able to see me through the drive-through panes, but I stayed hidden anyway.

Another person appeared a few steps away, in a similar state of shabby disarray. He stepped up to Timothy, who greeted him with a jerk of his chin. They spoke, but I couldn't hear. An exchange of something occurred right before the man picked up the brown bags, tucked them into a backpack, and left.

Timothy didn't budge.

The door to the Frolicking Moose opened, bells jostling as it swung wide into the room. With a start, I hurried back to the counter, relieved to see Dahlia and Bastian trail inside. Dahlia beamed, her fingers tangled in Bastian's.

"Good morning!"

"Are you sure you don't want me to cover for you?" I asked as I gratefully separated from the window. "I'm happy to work this afternoon."

She waved a hand. "Bash has emails to catch up on and he secretly wants to have a reason to stare at me all day."

A stormy, hot look from Bastian affirmed it. She winked at him as she tied an apron around her waist. I tugged at the string on the back of my apron, reluctant to leave. Would Bastian walk me to my car? Probably. I could stay here with them until Timothy left. The last thing I wanted was to be alone right now, and Vik was at work.

Then again, I might swing by The Outfitters and—

The door clanged open again, admitting Timothy's dark figure.

He strolled up to the counter before I could summon a

breath. The next second, he registered me standing there. His brow dropped into a heavy frown. Upper lip curled back, over his teeth.

Dahlia put a hand on my arm, holding me tight above the elbow. The thought that she must recognize him from the grocery store flittered through my mind, then back out. Staring at Timothy's back and comprehending all the havoc he'd wreaked on my life was one thing.

His glittering gaze, five steps away, was another.

The hidden malice from the other day lay abundantly clear now, though sprinkled with surprise. Given a guess, I'd say that he didn't expect to see me either. Small consolation.

If I'd just stepped around the counter, I could have acted like a customer and not an employee. Now he'd know that I worked here, and that was entirely too much for him to know.

I swallowed.

Timothy stopped at the counter, attention riveted on me. My stomach balled, filled with a leaden weight. I pulled my shoulders back and tried to slow my breaths. He'd already taken enough.

He would *not* take this moment.

But my voice wouldn't work. I opened my mouth to speak and could only stare. Thunder clapped in my mind. Rain pattered the ground. Gravel grated into my back, painfully sharp and—

"Kate," Timothy murmured. "Didn't expect to see you here."

His carefully neutral tone—not quite a greeting, not quite a question—sent a hum of fright through me. That voice. The edginess, filled with ridges and violence. The last time I'd heard it had been the trial, when he'd attempted to convince the judge that he was innocent.

What did he want?

Why stand here?

The sound of a moving chair scraping across the ground clued me into the world around us. I shook my head, yanked from the tunnel as Bastian strode over. His large body edged Timothy back from the counter and stood between the two of us. With Timothy's unreadable stare off of me, I shrank back.

"Time to go," Bastian said.

His tight shoulders and the coiled promise in his voice left no questions. Dahlia tugged me closer to her.

"C'mere," she murmured.

Timothy sidestepped when Bastian crowded him. "This doesn't involve you," Timothy sneered. His attention lingered on me for a moment longer before Bastian's towering body forced Timothy to step out of sight.

"It does now."

Bastian extended his arms, hands open in a silent, beckoning invitation. Timothy scuttled back like a scowling crab. His eyes flashed to mine once before he shoved back outside, muttering swear words under his breath. The door slammed behind him.

Dahlia put a firm arm around my waist.

"We've got you."

My heart slammed in my chest as I held onto her wrist with silent gratitude, squeezing. Timothy turned onto the sidewalk and disappeared down the road. I let out my first long, slow breath when I couldn't see him. My head whirled.

"Thank you," I whispered.

Once he confirmed Timothy wasn't coming back, Bastian turned around and eyed me.

"You good?"

I nodded.

Dahlia eyed me with concern, gazing between me and Bastian. An unspoken question lingered in the air, to which Bastian nodded. He glanced at his phone, then stuffed it back into his pocket.

"Vik is on his way." He straightened. "I'll keep an eye out until he shows up."

With that, Bastian stationed himself at the door, staring outside, arms folded over his chest.

Chapter Sixteen

VIKRAM

Four words on a text from Bastian compelled me to slam my car door and jog through the Frolicking Moose parking lot.

Bastian: Get to the shop.

The coffee shop lay uncannily quiet for the noon hour, the end of Kate's shift. My heart hammered at the thought that something must be wrong.

I stepped inside to find Bastian only a few steps away, surly as a bear. A scowl crossed his face, brows low over his eyes. Kate sat at a table, her purse on her lap. She'd wrapped her arms around it and hugged it to her chest. Dahlia glanced at me from where she stood at the drive-through, passing a cup through the window. Relief crossed her expression. Tension lay palpable in the air.

A questioning glance to Bastian only returned with a lifted eyebrow and head tilt to Kate. He shuffled back toward his computer in the far corner, but he didn't sit down. His gaze lingered out the window.

I stepped over to Kate.

"Kate?"

She startled, jerked out of a thought, and blinked at me. A trying smile appeared, then disappeared. She reached out, a hand on my wrist.

"Hey." She cleared her throat. "I'm sorry, I could have—"

"No. Don't do that. That's not what we do. Scoot over."

She shifted across the bench and I slid in. There wasn't much space, but I had a feeling she wanted it that way. Her thigh pressed up against mine. Her face pale, her color waning. She blinked several times, extricating from thoughts. I put my arm around the back of the bench, though I wanted to drop it to her shoulders.

"What's going on?" I asked gently.

Her head tilted back. A lock of hair tumbled onto her forehead, almost in her eyes. She swallowed.

"I . . . that is . . . ah . . ."

Kate sighed, her shoulders slumping. Her thick eyelashes fanned against her cheeks, hidden by glasses again. She picked at a string on her purse absently, as if she didn't even see it.

Her gaze meant mine, pleading. "Can we go somewhere else?" she asked. Her voice shook. "Somewhere where we can talk?"

Something told me this had nothing to do with our explosive first kiss, and everything to do with Timothy Hanover.

"Yes."

I held out my hand. She hesitated, then slowly slipped her fingers in mine. They braided together, palm to palm.

"I know just the spot."

* * *

My old family canoe rocked in the water.

The gentle stream we maneuvered through moseyed across a rocky canyon, rubbing along the edges of the rocks as it slipped by. Not a sound, not a white cap, not a soul.

Nothing lay around us except blue sky, dark water, and puffy clouds.

Kate hadn't said a word as I told her to get changed, loaded the canoe on top of the Jeep at my place, tossed the oars in the back, and drove to the river. We unloaded in the same stillness. In the movements, the lack of talking, her color returned. She seemed less gaunt, though distant.

If Kate wanted peace, then Kate needed water.

When I handed her a paddle, she wrapped her fingers around it with a trying smile. She climbed into the front. As we navigated away from the shore and into the gently-winding river, she trailed her fingers over the side. Sunshine warmed her bare shoulders. Her hair topped her head in a messy bun that I wanted to tug loose and watch tumble free.

Instead, I waited.

Twenty minutes into our adventure, when no other sign of life stirred in the sleepy timber that sprinkled the mountains on either side, Kate spun around. Her legs, long and tanned in the sunshine, stretched in front of her. One of her toes gently touched my ankle and sent a shiver through me. She hid behind a pair of sunglasses, but I sensed that they gave her courage.

"I owe you an explanation, Vik."

No, I wanted to say. *You don't owe anyone, anything.*

My breath caught. I said nothing. This was her moment to control.

Kate pulled her knees into her chest, folded her arms, and rested them on her bent legs. She looked at me as she said, "Five years ago, I was at my aunt's house. Visiting, just for a minute. I had a few papers for her to sign and . . . anyway, that's not important. I got pulled into her frightening orbit longer than I wanted, and by the time I went to leave, it was dark."

Trina, a willful, bitter kind of woman, flashed through my mind. Trina hadn't always been that way. As a child, I remembered her with warmth. She'd squirt the hose over the fence when we played outside and try to soak us in the summer. Over the years, she faded.

Then she left.

Despite knowing what came next in Kate's story, my shoulders tightened all the same. Her fingers turned into white-skinned machines, gripping her arms so hard they blanched.

"I left out the back door to avoid . . . some people that had come into the front," Kate continued, wooden now.

Her evasive words, and the tone in which she said them, painted a clear picture. *Some people* meant gamblers, many of them druggies. Trina had all kinds of people coming in and out of that place, at all times of the day, when she ran extensive and hidden gambling tournaments.

I leaned back, my attention riveted on her. Though I couldn't see her eyes, her tone said it all. She was far away, somewhere else.

"Timothy was in the back. I have no idea what he was doing back there. He called out to me, I ignored him. I didn't know him. I'd seen him at Trina's before but hadn't really spoken with him. He sort of gave me the creeps. Anyway, he followed me around the side."

"The far side of the house?"

She nodded. Trina lived behind my old house. Our backyards shared the far fence. On the other side of Trina's house was another house, dilapidated and old. A tired eyesore that the neighbors constantly complained about. Low lighting cast it in shadows, and thick bushes blocked much of it from view, particularly along the driveway that ran all the way to the back.

"It was storming," she murmured. "I . . . I guess I wasn't thinking. I just wanted out of there, so I ran. Timothy chased."

Vini's preparation, though lacking in detail, prepared me for what came next. She adjusted, set her chin on her folded arms.

"He tackled me from behind." She winced, jaw tight. "I still . . . I still remember the gravel scraping on my back. The dark bushes. The . . . thunder. I saw his face in a flash of lighting. Then . . ."

She trailed away.

I didn't move, worried I'd frighten her away. She had nowhere to go but the water, yet the rhythmic consistency of her voice told me that's exactly where she'd go next, given the opportunity.

"Then he raped me," she said simply.

The words came out unencumbered, as if she mentioned a grocery list, and I couldn't help but wonder how long it had taken her to get to that point. To be able to say such horrific words without a visible shudder, a sob.

"You pressed charges?" I asked quietly.

She nodded. "Called the cops, they came. Went to the ER, pressed charges, the whole deal. I don't think I would have gone through with it if Vini and Amma hadn't been there for me."

My nostrils flared. I'd been so in and out of the family, and they kept confidence so well, I hadn't even known. Disappearing into adventures, living my wild life. It cost me an opportunity to help someone who meant more to me than I knew was possible.

Words and thoughts flooded me, but I couldn't articulate any of them. A hot rock sat in my throat, blocking my brain. Flashes of the coiled, angry man that came into the Outfitters, looking for a job, trickled through my mind. His cagey eyes. Tightly-held body.

I forced myself to stop.

Kate gazed out over the river, chin held aloft. Sunlight brightened her bronzing skin, and a few tendrils of hair slipped out of a ponytail to fly around her temples.

"So," I murmured, "Timothy was released and you lost your rental."

She chuckled, but it had no humor. "Yes, which . . . brings us full circle."

"What happened today?"

Less robotically, with more confusion than understanding, she relayed the events. Seeing him at the lake, then inside. His approach, Bastian's interference. By the time she finished, her forehead formed deep grooves.

"I just . . . I don't think he knew I was in there. We seemed to surprise each other. But then he stayed. He said my name."

Her voice rang with fury now, as if Timothy had taken something away from her when he spoke.

I scoffed, leaning back. "You're being nicer than he deserves."

"Maybe," she murmured, fidgeting with the end of a strand of hair, "but I don't think so. I think he did something stupid in the back—dealt drugs or exchanged something or whatever—and then came in for a cup of coffee. His expression made it seem like he was as surprised as me, just like the grocery store."

"He may have assumed you moved on, away from here."

She sighed. "Perhaps I should have. We're bound to keep running into each other. Where is he going to go? Is this what we'll be doing from here on out? I can't live like this. It's . . . awful. I'll be looking for him around every corner."

"He should leave, not you."

She turned to me, chin propped on her hand. "What if he doesn't?"

"Then you always have me."

A long silence expanded between us, swelling like a living thing. Her nostrils flared. She swallowed, said nothing. Her lips parted slightly, then closed. I leaned forward, arms on my knees.

"Kate, I already knew."

Her head jerked up.

"What?"

I held up two hands. "Deductions and guesses, that's all. Vini didn't betray you, and neither did Amma. In fact, I was . . . pretty pissed that I hadn't heard earlier. That I couldn't have helped."

Her eyebrows crashed together. Another wordless silence

passed before she managed to say, "How?" Before I could answer, the consternation softened with understanding. "The anxiety attack at the store."

I nodded.

"I texted Hernandez about the man that Dahlia described standing behind you, and he told me about Timothy. I drew some parallels, called Vini, and she told me it wasn't her story to tell. That's it, but . . . it was pretty much confirmation."

Kate laughed, a sound I couldn't decode beyond incredulousness, frustration, or warmth.

"Sounds like Vini," she murmured. "She breathed me through it, you know? So did Amma, just like when I was a little girl. Especially the days right after. Amma and Appa brought me home, told my aunt. Appa bawled her out—she hasn't spoken to me since. Can't now," she added softly.

A realization dawned on me then. "Is that when Trina went to jail?"

Her jaw tightened as she nodded.

"Yes."

"Oh."

"Appa outed her gambling ring to the police afterward. I started going to therapy a few months later, with one of Vini's friends. Recovery felt like . . . a hurricane. Encompassing. Consuming. The whole event hit me from every side and I didn't know who I was anymore. A day or a week at a time, I pulled it back together. I'm a totally different person now. It . . . changed me irrevocably. I'll never be the same. But I've accepted now that I'm better. Stronger. I've proven what I can conquer."

"Lady warrior," I murmured.

She tilted her head back and laughed. "Lady warrior. I will take that title proudly."

"I'm sorry, Kate, that he took something that wasn't his, and that the bastard walks the streets again."

The uncertainty in the air fractured, relieving both of us. I reached for both oars and repositioned us in the silence that followed. When she offered nothing more, I said, "Thank you for trusting me with your story. I know that wasn't easy."

"Don't thank me yet," she murmured. "It's clearly not over. I just delayed the inevitable today."

"What do you mean?"

"Timothy and I will eventually have to face each other again, right? If I'm not willing to leave, and he doesn't seem to either, I can't just keep hiding from him. He's . . . angry. Livid. I can see it in him. We're going to keep bumping into each other until something explodes."

Water dripped off the oar as we spun slowly in the middle of the river. We'd stopped paddling, so we inched downstream. A fish bobbed to the top of the river nearby, gaping mouth gone in a gasp.

"Did you . . . I mean . . ." she trailed away with a light growl in the back of her throat. "I . . ." She pulled her sunglasses off and stared right at me. "Did you give me a space to live because you felt sorry for me?"

"No."

"Because you felt obligated?"

"No."

"Then why?"

The opportunity to hesitate presented itself, but I didn't take it. No, I owed her far more than that. The girl had just opened herself like an artery.

"Because I care about you. And to hell with you being my little sister, all right? That's not how this will work."

The response, emergent from the bottom of my gut, caused no reaction in her at first. She slipped the glasses back over her eyes. Her gaze turned to the river, smoothly rippling below. Chin in her hands, she faced me again. Her voice, quiet as the forest, fell in a hush.

"What does that mean, Vik?"

"It means I'll kill the bastard if he ever touches you again. That I'll keep you safe in whatever way that means to you. That I'm here for anything you need. Always."

A hint of defiance claimed her voice.

"I'm not broken."

I laughed. "You are the least broken person I've ever met. You're a diamond, not a shell."

"Did you kiss me back because you felt sorry for me?"

"What? No!"

"I'm not damaged goods or dirty or impure or unwholesome or any of that."

I shook my head. "No, you're not."

Her resistance faded. Guards lowered as she leaned back, hands on the edge of the canoe. The worst of her defensiveness melted.

"Okay," she murmured.

"What do you need from me, Kate?"

"I don't know. I don't know what he's going to do, or how this is going to happen. Kinoshi gave me the restraining order, but . . ."

She trailed away. Any legal protection comforted me more than none, but I still didn't know what that would mean. Timothy didn't show active pursuit against her, but that gave no reassurance.

I would never trust this guy.

"Whatever it is." I pulled gently on one of the oars. "I'm always here."

Kate stared out at the forest and didn't say another word.

* * *

The flickering screen of a monster movie flashed through the darkness of my house later that night. An open window spilled cooling summer air into the room, washing away the sterile smell of the air conditioner. The salty-sweet tang of fresh popcorn drifted by on a breeze.

Light filtered through from the kitchen, which I'd left on to keep the house from getting too dark. Kate lounged at my side, close but not touching. The rest of the day had been filled with contemplative silence. We ate dinner together on the back porch, underneath the umbrella, but said not much at all.

The quiet held no burden.

Space to think through what she said only led to the same conclusions as before: I'd protect her. A hardening of my resolve naturally followed. I'd be there for her in ways no one else ever had.

If she let me.

A careful distance lived in her eyes now. She didn't avoid me, but she didn't move close. The smell of her shampoo drifted to me every now and then. I tried to ignore it, relieved that she was safe.

Here.

The movie faded by. I comprehended none of it. My thoughts churned in the background, spinning in ways I didn't try to track. The sound of a sigh brought me out of them. I glanced over to find her leaning against the back of the couch, eyes closed. She'd pulled a blanket over her shoulder, but it fell off. Her sooty eyelashes fluttered against her cheek, rosy from the sunshine.

With an adorable little yawn, she scooted closer, rested her head on my shoulder, and dropped into sleep.

I froze, then leaned in.

"Always, Kate," I whispered. "Always."

Chapter Seventeen

KATELYN

The smell of lemongrass settled me further into my body.

I drew in a deep breath of hot humid air, let it back out, and tried to enjoy the elongation of my thigh. Heat swelled in and out of my lungs, loosening tension all the way at my core.

"Hold for two more breaths."

A dainty yoga instructor sauntered past, bare feet quiet on the wooden floor that creaked as he walked by. To my right, I was vaguely aware of Vikram in full dolphin pose, his right arm trembling as it held the weight of his body. I mentally set him aside for the tenth time.

Days had passed since our soul-stirring canoe trip. The water, the quiet, the stillness had given me courage I may not have thought possible before. Having the secret out made it easier to exist, a physical weight unburdened. In a small way, we'd shoved the kiss out of the way again. Thankfully, we didn't speak about either the kiss or Timothy.

Rule number five, *never speak about what happened,* remained on alert. I didn't want to discuss either of them with Vikram, and he didn't ask any questions.

Vikram's calm acceptance of my sordid experiences, the fact that he'd already known, made it easier to move on. He'd known and he hadn't run. Hadn't avoided me. Hadn't treated me any differently than before.

Now, he walked a little closer, kept a hand on the small of my back in public, and tracked our surroundings more deeply. His vague touches didn't feel suffocating, but sent frissons of deep emotion all through my body.

This isn't real, I reminded myself daily.

Vikram didn't commit.

Sweat dripped down my arms as we moved into child's pose. My muscles lolled gratefully. Each released breath, I pictured inky smoke escaping my body, never to return.

When the class ended, the teacher opened a side door. Air swept through the sultry room. Sweat saturated my shirt, which clung to my ribs when Vikram walked up, water bottle held out for me. I thanked him, popped the top, and had a long drink. The cool, refreshing liquid eased my parched throat.

"Like the class?" he asked.

"Very much. How did your knee do?"

He bent it, face studious. "Not bad. Had to modify most of them, but it feels good to get back in here. Thanks for coming. I needed it."

"I enjoyed it, too."

His gaze dropped to my lips, then away. He swallowed, throat bobbing. I pushed the water bottle into his hand.

"This was, by far, my favorite class," he continued. "Having you here changed everything."

Before I could dissect that loaded statement—he'd been to this class at least twenty times—a woman approached. She had a sweet smile and low-slung eyelids. Her slightly flattened nose gave her a charming, girlish appearance.

"Hey, Vik."

He dropped into the familiar wooden smile I'd come to expect when approached by other women.

"Hey, Zara. How are you?"

She pushed hair off her sticky shoulders with a brightening smile. "Doing great. So good to see you here again. I heard you had surgery?"

He nodded. "Recovering well, now. Had to use some modifications but I'm feeling good."

The urge to flee nearly overcame me, but I remained rooted to the spot when Zara glanced at me. Too late, a smile came to her face. Calculation—perhaps some vague question—lingered in her eyes.

Good heavens.

This woman just sized me up.

"Are you busy after this?" Zara asked. Her fingertips lingered near his elbow. "I thought it might be fun to grab a smoothie, like we used to. What do you think?"

I stepped back, prepared to get out of his way, but an arm came around my waist. The pressure of his hand on my hip made my breath catch.

"Not today, sorry Zara. Thank you, though."

A crestfallen expression followed but she smiled, sent me an appraising glance, and flounced away. Vik didn't look me in the eye. My heart thumped painfully.

"Ready to go?"

I nodded, unable to speak around the jumble of emotions heavy on my chest. Zara hadn't even tried to hide her simmering jealousy. Yet, the simper of a flattered woman evaded me. Instead, a question: how many other women would there be?

Had there been?

Vik gathered his things, dodged questions from other people with his usual smooth smile, and ushered me out. Heat baked off the sidewalk in sticky waves, cooler than the bikram yoga class we left behind. The prickling warmth subsided as a fresh breeze blew past. Vikram's fingers brushed against mine as he reached back for his car keys. A fleeting breath, and I thought he'd grab my hand. His fingers skimmed right past.

Disappointment keened.

He ebbed and flowed. Made a statement, fell back.

Did *he* even know what he wanted?

An awkward air filled the car as we climbed inside the Jeep. Words choked my throat. These moments served as solid reminders of who Vik was—or had been—and how that interacted with his daily life now. Those thoughts didn't linger for long. If anyone knew that the past could be overcome, I did.

"Does that happen often?" I asked quietly.

He tilted his head against the seat as we idled at a stoplight. He blinked, then flipped on the blinker and turned down a different road.

"All the time."

"Do you get tired of it?"

"I do now."

"You used to like it?"

Reluctantly, he nodded. "Yes, but now it's . . . I don't know. Zara and I are friends, that's it."

My mouth opened, but the question wouldn't slip out. *What changed? Why do you look so torn up?* Somehow, I felt it wasn't my place. I turned to look out the window, closed my eyes, and let the flapping breeze cool my fevered skin.

I'd never be friends with Vik.

All or nothing, that was all it could ever be. I'd been too in love with him, for far too long, to dance around it with friendship. Living with him had only drawn the line more firmly in the sand.

Would he deal with that?

He hadn't in the past. Commitment? He ghosted. No reason to stay, no risk to take. Yet, people changed all the time.

"Do you regret it?" I asked.

He turned to me in a glance as quick as hummingbird wings. In the fleeting thing, I could see that he knew what I really asked. *That lifestyle, was it really worth it?* Hair fluttered over my face, dancing across my eyes. His fingers tightened on the steering wheel.

"All the time."

"Are there any of the women that you miss?"

"None."

I swallowed. He spoke more definitively than I'd expected. Maybe that's what I'd feared. In all these years, he'd never attached enough to say goodbye, so what made this situation special?

Why would I be any different?

If I lost Vik, I could lose everything.

As if he read my mind, Vik reached over, grabbed my hand, and threaded his fingers through mine. My breath stopped. I held it in my chest, waiting to see how it would feel if I didn't pull away. It seemed to make a statement when I did nothing.

The lonely little girl in me sat up and took notice. *It's happening,* she thought. The long feel of his fingers, soft and firm at the same time, was exactly what I had always imagined they would be.

Finally, when I could stand it no longer, I tightened my hold on his fingers with a light squeeze, then turned my face to the breeze. Vik gave no explanation and no answers. Would it be fair to ask it of him? Not now. We all had demons to face. He hadn't left me alone when I faced mine.

I wouldn't abandon him either.

* * *

An angry bellow woke me out of a dead sleep.

I gasped awake, upright in bed. Covers pooled around my waist. Humidity lay in the air, thick. Outside, lightning flashed, crackling across an ominously dark skyline. A blast of air conditioning danced over the top of my skin, cooling the sweat I'd broken into.

Dreams.

Nightmares.

With a groan, I shoved out of bed. Walking back and forth across the room oriented me out of the sticky tendrils of dark dreams. Something in the *thud* of my feet on the floor broke loose the uncertainty, oriented me in the now. A distant clap of thunder, more roll than bang, made me flinch. The sporadic *tick, tick, tick* of raindrops hitting the window set my teeth on edge. A growl sounded in my ears.

I grimaced.

"Not real." My thumb pressed into my pointer finger. "It's just a dream. I'm safe. I'm home. Timothy is not waiting in the shadows."

Lightning branched through the air, illuminating the umbra. I swallowed past a distant scream, the memory of my own. To assist my return to what was real, I flipped on a lamp. Opened my closet, nudged the door to the hall wider so I could see behind it.

No monsters.

Just the ones in my head.

Damn the storm. Damn Timothy. I'd done so well. Slept through countless thunderstorms the last year or two. Of course he'd haunt me now, when I had a hope of disappearing into the horizon with him at my back.

Kinoshi's manilla envelope lay in my drawer, hidden under all my pajamas. It still called to me, a taunting thing.

Reminders.

So many reminders.

Despair followed. Though I felt myself firmly oriented in the moment, I loathed these problems. One drunk, drug-addled decision on Timothy's part and the rest of my life had been utterly changed.

Bitterness crept back in. For years, I'd managed to chew through it. Get rid of each piece as it rose. Now, Timothy walked free and I didn't. He set my life off-kilter *again*.

I grabbed a blanket, wrapped myself in it, and stalked to the front room. Vikram's door lay canted open, his breaths quiet and gentle as I slipped by. I resisted the urge to climb into bed with him and plowed into the living room instead.

The clock declared the time as a ripe 2:56. It would be almost 5:00 am for Vinita. The temptation to text her followed. She'd always been a late sleeper, though. 5:00 am was unfathomable to her unless work required it. Since she set her own hours, her clients never required such a timeframe.

No.

This I could do on my own.

I *needed* to do this on my own.

The storm grumbled in the background when I flipped on the TV. Vikram had seven channels, but nothing appealed. The dull drone of late-night shows made the agitation worse. I jumped with a squeak when a boom descended on the mountains. The windows trembled.

"Holy coconuts," I muttered.

Hail bounced like hot popcorn on the road outside, leaping all over the place. I double-checked the locked front door, then the back door. A cup of tea, another warm blanket, several minutes of pacing, a lamp or two, and an abandoned attempt to eat later, it all felt worse.

"I've got this," I murmured. "I can do this."

There had been plenty of thunderstorms in the early days of traumatic recovery, when I'd slept in Vini's bed. Later, I struggled through them on my own. None of them had been this percussive, however. The noise was so deafening. Hail slammed into the roof with violence, as if the storm wanted to lash through the walls.

When another clap of thunder jump-started my heart again, I dropped the blankets and hurried down the hall.

Forget this.

I didn't *have* to be alone anymore.

Vikram lay on his stomach, sprawled in the middle of the bed. Rain sluiced down the windows in shadows when I crept to the other side. His room smelled like lemongrass and dried sage, a heady mixture that made me think of him. Lightning illuminated the path around his bed.

"Vik?" I murmured. I eased onto the bed next to him. He stirred, sleepy. Near him, the binding tension in my chest began to unwind. Dangerous ground, to steady myself to him so quickly.

While the storm continued to fuss, I tugged on his blankets. "Vik?"

His head lifted in a sleepy, one-eye-opened daze. He blinked, saw me, and pushed onto his elbows.

"Kate?"

"I, uh . . ." I swallowed. Sweet baby pineapple, how did a grown woman tell the love of her life that she was frightened of *thunder*? "I—"

A burst of illumination broke outside, followed by an immediate crack. I jolted. In an instant, his warm hand clamped around my arm. His silky voice tugged my heart.

"C'mere, lady."

The next moment, I lay tucked against his chest. He curled an arm around me, pulling me close. His body felt lean and toasty, his power encompassing. He lifted the blankets, brought them over me, and used a hand to brush aside my hair. When he settled with a little sigh, goosebumps broke across the back of my neck.

I snuggled deeper.

He tightened his hold.

Fear swept away. The storm surged. Lightning broke. Thunder sang. The rain dropped in buckets. My heart settled into low waves of relief. A tear rolled down my cheek, dropped onto the pillow, and faded with the rest of my revenants.

Into sweet, sweet oblivion.

VIKRAM

A note lay on top of my pillow.

I stared at it, uncertain whether I should leave it, or just wake Kate up. After spooning her half the night, it felt wrong to leave her in bed alone. A note would soften my escape, I hoped, so she didn't feel abandoned.

The warm covers, the delicious feel of her against me, beckoned.

Stupid job.

Waking her would be ridiculous with darkness bruising the skin under her eyes. Clearly, she hadn't slept much, and today was her only day off. How long had she been awake before she came into my room with that helluva storm?

Who knew.

Her palpable anxiety worried me. The quiet, pleading way she'd said my name, as if she didn't want to bother me but couldn't stop herself. The moment I awoke to her poised meekly nearby, and thunder in the background, Vini's warning had woken in my mind.

Thunderstorms and darkness are her two biggest triggers.

Holding her close all night had been no hardship, particularly after our shared yoga class and her patience with me. I'd turned into a mellow, sulky grump afterward. The urge to stay nearly kept me here instead of going into work. The desire to protect her welled up from deep within.

"I can protect you," I murmured, "but I don't know if I can promise more than that."

She slept on.

I brushed a lock of hair out of her face. I'd never hesitated to leave a sleeping woman before, Kate had been such a refreshing difference from the beginning. A quizzical study of firsts. A beep on my watch indicating the hour spurred me along. Given the chance, I'd study her sleeping for days.

I had to go.

With one last kiss to her temple, I murmured, "Always," and slipped out the door.

* * *

The smell of BBQ drifted in the air.

I lifted my nose, breathing deep of brisket and char, and let it whoosh back out. While I didn't consume meat more than a few times a week, I never refused a Dagny brisket.

Blades of green grass shot out of the lawn in Hernandez's backyard, where a small crowd congregated. Dagny stood by a smoker, which belched a steady haze into the summery air. Dahlia sprawled on a folding chair nearby, face tilted back to soak in the sunshine. Bastian sat next to her, his massive hand clamped around her small fingers. She chattered, content, while Dagny laughed. Bastian didn't have to say a word.

Dahlia was perfect for him.

I pushed the screen door closed, drawing their attention. Dahlia brightened like a lit firecracker. Dagny grinned.

"Hey V-vik," she called. "Over here."

I passed a table laden with Hernandez's favorite ale, some

sparkling waters, a mixture of pop cans, and gleaming ice. I plucked a sparkling water out of the bucket and headed their way. Heat rippled off the cement patio as I gave Dagny a hug. Her eyes sparkled as she pulled away.

"It's so g-good to see you again, and looking m-much healthier than what J-jayson said."

I chuckled. "Definitely feeling better."

Her gaze darted behind me. Her lips pulled into a frown. "Where's Kate? She's c-coming, right?"

"In a few minutes. She's closing the coffee shop today."

"Oh, good. I'm so excited to g-get to know her better. How is your kn-nee?"

"Good. Almost three months out of surgery. I'm still only cleared to work part-time, but that's better than sitting in my house."

Dagny's smile widened. "I'm h-h-happy to hear you've rejoined the l-land of the living." Her tone dropped so only I could hear, and she squeezed my arm gently. "We've b-been so worried about you. K-kate, it sounds like, has been a g-good thing in your life."

"The best," I instantly replied. The truth of it sank all the way to my chest. Kate wasn't a *good thing in my life.*

She was everything.

The thought hit like a meteor right in my chest, leaving my heart gasping in its wake. I shoved it aside to think about later, but knew I'd chew on it for hours. Dahlia twiddled her fingers in a wave. Bastian gave me a quick head jerk in greeting. Sunglasses hid his eyes. I cracked open the sparkling water, then had a tangy sip of grapefruit.

"Where's Hernandez?" I asked.

"Working t-today, but just f-finishing up his shift, I think," Dagny murmured. "He c-called when he was headed h-home, said he had to grab a theft r-r-report before he signed off."

"So," Dahlia drawled with a white-toothed grin. "How are things, Vik?"

"Don't ask me like that."

Innocence crossed her face. "Like what? It's just a question."

I shot her a glare.

Her smile widened.

Dahlia posed as a potential ally for me in my attempts to get Kate to trust me in more than a physical sense, but I wasn't ready to commit to Dahlia as a cohort yet.

I hadn't seen Kate since last night, when she'd fallen asleep on the couch listening to an audiobook. Recalling her soft, wispy breaths, and the way she turned limp as a noodle, filled me with the same incomprehensible sensation I'd never experienced before. Was it love?

All I could say is that I knew I'd do anything for her. I swallowed a rising heartbeat. That girl affected me in strange ways. Heartburn. Palpitations. If this *was* love, which I wasn't ready to commit to yet but couldn't exactly laugh off as impossible, then love hurt.

"How's physical therapy?" Bastian asked.

"Good." I bent the knee, grateful that it felt loose and easy. "Making a lot of progress. Started lifting weights again. Simple, light stuff. I've been able to reintegrate gentle yoga poses back in that I've missed."

Bastian nodded.

A few minutes of small talk later, the back door slammed open. Hernandez stepped outside in full sheriff's deputy kit, complete with taser and earpiece radio. He jerked a head nod to me, Bastian, said hello to Dahlia, then skimmed past everyone and slammed a kiss on Dagny's lips that would have frightened a lesser woman.

I looked away.

Bloody hell, but my friends were show-offs.

Hernandez smacked Dagny in the butt after he pulled away.

"Just had to let you know I'm home," he said. "I'll go get changed. How much longer until it's ready?"

"Thirty m-minutes."

"Perfect."

He strode toward me with a quick clap on the shoulder. "Gotta go change inside," he said. "Come with me. We need to talk."

An undercurrent in his tone propelled me after him. A cool blast of air conditioning greeted us as we stepped inside, closing the door behind us. Hernandez stood by the table while he ripped off his tactical belt. His brown eyes found mine.

"Thought I should warn you."

My entire body tensed. "Oh?"

"Your boy, Timothy? He's suspected on some burglary charges. There's been someone going around, taking things out of garages, unlocked cars, that kind of thing."

"How do you know it's him?"

"Video footage."

My good mood dimmed considerably. "I see."

Hernandez straightened up, setting aside a pair of handcuffs on his growing pile of stuff as he pulled it off. "We have two videos with him in it. It's clearly him, from identifying t-shirts to facial recognition. One from inside, one from a garage that he entered without permission. Now he's escalated."

"He broke into a house?"

Hernandez nodded. I bit back a curse.

"I see."

"It gets worse." He grimaced and sat down to unlace a boot. "They're houses he's clearly staked out. It started with wealthier people, you know? He's taking the quick, easy stuff out of cars. Jewelry, tablets, watches, that kind of thing. Today, he got stupid, as we like to say."

"How?"

"Held a knife to a homeowner and threatened to kill them

while raiding a jewelry box. Luckily, we have the whole thing on camera, with audio."

"Isn't that a violation of parole or something?"

He snorted. "Major violation. If we could find him. He's gone missing the last twenty-four hours. Hasn't checked in."

"Damn."

"There's no sign of him near your place that I can tell. At least, none of the reports have happened near you, but you might want to keep an eye out. He's desperate, yet hasn't shown any signs of being vengeful toward Kate. Not that I can tell, anyway. I think he'll lay low for a while, then try to get out of here. If he's not already gone. Man would be a fool for sticking around after his last stint, but I can't say that people are always bright."

"Him leaving for good," I muttered, "would be the second-best thing. If he never came back, I'd be a happy man."

The first-best thing would be Timothy walking himself off a very high cliff.

"Does Kate have my direct cell?" Hernandez asked.

"No."

"Get it in her phone so she can call me if she needs anything, even if I'm off duty."

"Thanks."

Hernandez studied me, then nodded. "I like her. So what's your problem?"

I scowled. "Not your business."

His grin grew. "C'mon, amigo. It *is* my business. I'm a happily married man! *Abuela* finally likes me again and I want all my brothers to be happy too. You're the only one left, anyway. Dagny is going to make it her business if you're not careful."

I sighed. "I'm working it out."

Hernandez yanked his vest off. "Well don't be an idiot while you're trying to figure it out, all right? In my line of work, it's the idiots that come in last."

A rap on the front door drew my attention. I glanced up, waved to Hernandez to indicate I'd open the door, and crossed the kitchen. Kate stood on the porch, eyes darting around the neighborhood. Relief rushed through me when I saw her. Unable to help myself, I reached out, grabbed her arm, and yanked her inside. She landed against my chest with an *oomph*.

"Hello," she murmured, close to my neck.

I kept a firm hold on her, probably for too long, before I pulled away. She peered up at me, surprise in her gaze.

"You good?" she asked.

"Yes, now I am."

The desire to kiss her again was a physical thing I had to wrestle back, out of power. Two weeks had passed since she'd laid that kiss on me and rocked my metaphorical world.

I still thought about it all the time.

I released her. Hernandez appeared in the doorway between rooms.

"Hey, Kate," he called. She smiled, but didn't move away from me. I wanted to draw her in, drinking her like a cold glass of water. News of Timothy had shaken me up. No part of me feared *that* idiot. I could handle him with a bad knee and on a bad day. But I did fear for Kate.

For her comfort.

Her presence of mind.

Hernandez had given me a few minutes of reaction time to come to terms with what he'd just revealed, which I appreciated. A few deep breaths, and seeing her safe in front of me, restored my ability to think this through.

Before she could move away, I hooked an arm around her shoulders and steered her toward the hallway.

"C'mere," I murmured. "We gotta talk."

To the right of the hall was a small, spare bedroom. I ducked inside and closed the door. Light streamed through the window, illuminating pale peach walls and plush carpet. Supplies and bookshelves filled it. Unopened oil stain containers. Plastic organizers with hammers, screws, nails. Blueprints. Dagny used this as a storage room for her side hobby building furniture out of palette wood. She only made a few pieces a year now, in between working her full-time construction management job out of Jackson City.

Apprehension filled Kate's face as she studied me, eyes wide. "Vik?"

"Hernandez just said that Timothy has a new warrant out for his arrest."

She sucked in a sharp breath.

"What for? What has he done?"

Quick as I could, I summarized his report. Kate listened, wordless, until I finished on a long breath. "Timothy hasn't checked in for over twenty-four hours."

Kate swallowed. "Oh."

She'd paled, but her calm mien was largely unchanged. A few moments passed in silence before she met my gaze again.

"Thank you for telling me. I'll thank Hernandez too."

"Let's come up with a plan," I said, a hand on her waist. "We'll make sure you're not home alone, all right? You can hang out with me and Daniel while I work, or I can come to the coffee shop until you're done if Bastian isn't already there."

Her brow creased. She folded her arms across her middle and dropped her gaze. "I can't ask that of you, Vik."

I reached out, tugged a hand free, and threaded our fingers together. "You didn't and I want to. Frankly, Kate, any reason to spend more time with you is a welcome one. If it happens to keep you safe from that bastard? All the better."

She blinked, eyes locked on our intertwined fingers. Her head lifted to stare right at me.

"Do you mean that?"

I reached deep, found the truth all the way in my middle soul, and whispered, "Every part of it."

Her mouth parted, then closed. She nodded.

"Okay."

"He's going to be found, Kate," I said with a reassuring squeeze. "Hernandez and the whole county will be watching for him, not to mention the police in Jackson City and other rural areas. Eventually, he'll get taken in and you'll be able to breathe free for a long, long time."

Kate's shoulders expanded under a deep breath. Then, in a move so shocking I could only stand frozen, she stepped into my space and wrapped her arms around my waist. Her heartbeat mingled with mine. The wispy sensation of her breath racing across my collarbone sent my head into a whirl.

I loved her.

I knew it.

The relief and rightness of clutching her to me, shirt fisted in my hands, could only be love. This nauseating, terrifying elation. The ability to do anything because she stood nearby. The hope for a future brighter than the past.

The words locked in my throat as I tightened my arm around her shoulders. She snuggled close when I anchored her in. Hernandez' voice floated through my mind, filled with exasperation.

So what's your problem?

I had no idea why a ball lodged in my throat. Why my heart raced in terror, my mind spun back, back, back, but didn't land on anything except pulpy pain and darkness. Kate had given me no reason to fear, yet I did.

I loved this woman.

That scared the courage to admit it out loud right out of me, because I couldn't be certain that love was enough.

"I hope you're right," she whispered. "Thank you, Vik."

"They'll get him, Kate," I murmured, rubbing my palm against her back in a gesture that soothed me more than her. "And when that happens? I'll be at your side the whole time."

* * *

The sizzle of fresh-grilled corn-on-the-cob, buttery rolls, and fresh-sliced watermelon tempted us back outside. Our fingers remained firmly locked together as I tugged Kate into the backyard. The tension in her shoulders eased as the bright sunshine hit us. I surveyed the yard.

Hernandez had changed into a loose pair of basketball shorts, flip flops, and a white t-shirt. He stood next to Dagny at the smoker, a hand on her hip. She gave him an adoring smile, then laughed at something Dahlia said. Hernandez threw an oven mitt at Dahlia, who giggled.

Bastian quirked an eyebrow at him in warning.

"Kaaaate!" Dahlia cried. "The party has finally arrived!"

Dagny's gaze dropped to our intertwined hands, then back to me with a knowing grin. I ignored her, but had a feeling I wouldn't be able to fend her off for much longer. Dahlia shot to her feet, wrapped an arm around Kate, and pulled her to a cluster of chairs near the smoker. Dagny dropped into one next to Kate and the three of them leaned forward, giggling like a bunch of hens.

Bastian eyed me as I returned, grabbed my open sparkling water, and chugged half the can. It burned all the way to my chest. Far too often, I wished I still drank the harder stuff.

"So," Bastian drawled.

"Shut up," I muttered.

He laughed, deep and rolling. Hernandez chortled from near the smoker.

After an easy silence where I let my thoughts unroll, and the sound of laughing children and a sprinkler issued from the other side of the fence, Hernandez settled on a lawn chair next to me.

"She good?" he asked.

"She'll be fine."

"I told Bastian." Hernandez nodded to him. "He's going to work from the Frolicking Moose and keep an eye out."

I met Bastian's gaze. "Thanks."

He gave a brief nod, raised his glass, then had a pull of ale.

Hernandez leaned back. "We'll get him, my friend. In the meantime, pay attention. He can't go that far with as few resources as he has now."

For some reason, the confidence in his tone didn't reassure me.

Chapter Nineteen

KATELYN

Vikram's words haunted me later that week.

Frankly, Kate, any reason to spend more time with you is a welcome one. If it happens to keep you safe from that bastard? All the better.

My traitorous heart gave into the fluttering sensation he inspired yet again, though I tried to hold back. He tugged my heartstrings with animalistic ferocity and he didn't even *know* it.

Talk about power.

Far too much power.

And strength.

Courage.

Power.

Whoops, back to that word again.

A basket of laundry spilled onto the couch when I dumped it out, my mind far from home. Wait, no. This wasn't my home. This was Vik's home. Yet, that didn't feel right either. Somehow in the intervening months, it had begun to feel like *my* home. Which wasn't far off, considering how much time I'd spent with his family over the years.

With a violent sigh, I snatched a towel off the top of the pile and folded it into half, then fourths. I eyed the clock. Vik would be home soon. Our shifts ended within thirty minutes of each other, so I'd come right home to wait for him. His concern for my life with Timothy on the loose had been so sweet. Reassuring.

With Vikram, I truly *wasn't* alone.

Frankly, I feared Timothy less than Vik these days. Vik tromped around with my heart and didn't even realize it. I shook my head.

No, that wasn't entirely true either.

After our surprise kiss, he must know he had it. The question was what he'd do with it by the end. He'd made no move, and neither had I. Either both of us held reservations we hadn't settled, or neither of us wanted to move forward. He'd been unusually quiet—and touchy—after the BBQ, but I couldn't peg why.

By the time I finished folding and replacing the laundry, the jittery feeling under my skin had subsided. I glanced out the back window, to the mountain vista's beyond, and gave into a little smile.

The BBQ had been a riot. Not only were Dagny and Dahlia two of my favorite women in Pineville, but they'd made me feel so at home. Like I really did belong with them, though Vik wasn't mine. He stood at my side often. His gaze found mine to check in with silent questions. Every now and then, he'd touch the small of my back, murmur something low. But I still held no official claim. He hedged his bets, drew closer, but said nothing concrete.

Watching Dagny and Hernandez dance around each other, eyes bright with affection, activated something scarred inside. A longing I hadn't truly let myself acknowledge in years. No, I'd been so wrapped up in rules and fears and control that I hadn't seen how rigid the structure of my life had become.

I sank to the couch, phone in hand, but didn't see the screen.

My thoughts drifted back to when I first saw Vikram months ago. Those rules had formed rigid walls in my brain, creating safety. Now, I had to step back and ask if they really *did* create safety.

In some regard, yes.

In others . . . no.

Wasn't it all just an illusion, anyway?

I set my phone aside, tilted my head back, and closed my eyes. Vikram gave me far too much introspection these days. The urge to call Vini and talk it out with her swept through me, but I shoved it aside. No, she didn't need the drama of the back-and-forth between me and her brother. We walked precarious ledges. She'd be too tempted to call her brother and smack him upside the head.

She'd certainly done it before.

Sleep stole over me as I crept deeper into my thoughts. With a little breath, I curled into a ball to escape the air conditioning, tucked my head against the couch, and let it take me away.

* * *

A high-pitched sound woke me hours later.

I startled awake with a gasp. Night had fallen, coating the room in shadows. Outside, lights winked near the reservoir. Fires in campgrounds, mostly, though some ambient illumination from cabins dotted the far mountainscape.

I pushed up.

What was that noise?

The irritating sound came from near my left thigh. With a groan, I grabbed my ringing phone and answered.

"'Lo?"

Vikram's frantic voice issued next. "Kate?"

"Yeah. Sorry. I was . . . asleep."

"You're all right?"

"Fine." I yawned, shoving hair out of my eyes. "I . . . dozed off, I think, after doing laundry."

He let out a long breath. "I've been so worried. I've called three times in the last hour. When you didn't answer I . . ."

I grimaced. "I'm sorry, Vik. I didn't hear it until just now. Everything is fine."

A pause filled the phone, one I wasn't sure how to tackle. Without being able to see his expression, I had no prayer of reading what he thought. His eyes were, truly, the windows to his fathomless soul.

"Vik?"

"It's fine," he grumbled. "I was worried."

"I appreciate that, and I'm sorry again."

"I'll be home in a few."

The call ended, and I dropped my phone back into my lap. His irritation wasn't my favorite way to wake up, but I couldn't say it hadn't happened before. Vik had a funny way of showing he cared through sheer annoyance.

Besides, why wasn't he home already? He was supposed to be here hours ago. By the time I gathered my brain back together, used the bathroom, tied my hair back, and shuffled into the living room in a pair of sweats and an old t-shirt, the sound of a car door closing came from outside. I folded myself back onto the couch with a wary eye on the door.

What to expect?

Vik pushed inside, shut the door behind him, and eyed me. The lock flipped, sealing us inside.

"Hey," he ventured.

Lines of stress filled his forehead, and an expression I couldn't hope to read. I held one hand to my face, sleeve pulled over my hand as if my fingers were cold.

"Hey," I murmured.

He eyed me. "You good?"

"Are you mad?" I countered.

"No. Are you?"

I shook my head. Though he promised he wasn't upset, he looked like a wary cat. He stepped away from the door, a brown bag rustling in his hands. He lowered to the couch and set the bag in front of me, as if it contained something fragile.

"I'm sorry if I came on too strongly on the phone." His contrite gaze met mine. "I was worried about you, that's all. The girl coming in after me canceled at the last minute, so I had to stay and help Daniel cover a two-hour lull. I called to let you know but . . . anyway. With Timothy still on the loose, I just want you to be safe."

"I know."

He gestured to the bag. "A peace offering?"

Curious, I leaned forward to peer inside. Plastic reflected the light back at first until I reached inside, dug it out, and studied it. Incredulous, my gaze lifted to his.

"A fishing starter kit?"

He grinned. "I thought you might want to come with me tomorrow. I haven't been in awhile and last time I went I wasn't all that sober. I'd like to rewrite some memories and do something fun together."

I blinked.

Not sober while fishing? The possibilities for disaster were endless.

"Fish," I repeated. "Like, the things that live in streams and bob their mouths open and closed and smell stinky when left in the sun?"

"Yes," he drawled, making a fishy face. I laughed, unable to help myself. The idea of getting my fingers on their squirmy, scaly bodies, oddly supple under all those shimmering scales, didn't appeal. But his earnest hope, and the sense that he wanted me to be excited about this idea, pushed me to smile.

Commitment to me or not, I was useless putty in Vikram's hands.

"That sounds fun, Vik."

"Great!" He clapped his hands together. "Tomorrow? It's your day off, right?"

"Right."

He stood, arms stretching over his head. The elongation lifted his shirt, revealing his abs. I quickly glanced away, desperately searching for something *else* to focus on.

"How was your day?" I asked, picking at the edge of the box. Lures and string and small scissors populated the interior, distracting me until his arms dropped back to the side. He groaned.

"No sign of Timothy from me, Hernandez, or Bastian," he murmured. He stepped back, then gripped the door jamb above the kitchen doorway. The space around my heart squeezed when he gripped the top and executed a perfect pull up. His arms bulged. The movement appeared effortless as he rattled on about impatient customers, the difficulties of working retail long-term, and why he hadn't started stock investments yet.

Sometimes, Vik had words he needed to just . . . get out.

Luckily, he didn't seem to expect a response while prattling about day trading as a new avenue of income. I ushered away all the other thoughts and gave up on following his stream of consciousness. The flex and pull of his arms as he lifted himself up and down thoroughly diverted me.

When I couldn't stand another second, I shot to my feet.

"Dinner?" I asked, setting the fishing kit back into the bag. Vik dropped, then smiled.

"And a movie?" he drawled.

My stomach caught. Something in the coded tone told me he wanted more than just to eat together. Vik wanted to snuggle. His daily touch quota clearly hadn't been filled, and I longed to snuggle into his side and watch something mindless.

Could my heart take it?

"Sure," I said to avoid a burdened silence.

He made a face. "Why do you sound like I just invited you to a zombie potluck?"

I burst out laughing. "Where did you come up with that?"

"Greatness. It's born in me."

The arrogant flip of his smile loosened my agitation. Wasn't that life with Vik? Uncertain one moment, charming the next. I felt like I constantly flailed around, trying to get a grip on something tenuous.

Time for total honesty.

"I do want to snuggle, Vik. Really. I just . . . I feel hesitant because I think it means something different for me than it does for you."

His expression immediately sobered.

"Like what?"

I pulled in a breath. "When I let someone be that physically close, it means I trust them. I can't help but feel a deeper sort of attachment or bond or . . ."

Alarm bells rang in my head. *Don't make me say it,* I silently pleaded. *Don't make me admit the thing that gives you all the power.*

Vik stepped closer, brow furrowed in concern. He reached up, a hand on my cheek. It sent a spiral of heat all the way through my fingertips.

"Hey," he murmured. "You have no reason to be scared."

"Do I look scared?"

"Terrified."

A quick mental check confirmed that he was, indeed, correct. "I am," I admitted, silently tacking on, *You don't know your power.*

"Of me?"

I paused, but not because it was true. I didn't know how to avoid saying what had to come next. If Vikram knew the depths of my admiration for him, he'd run a thousand miles away.

With the silence, Vik's concern deepened. He stepped back, giving me space.

"Kate, you—"

"I'm not afraid of you, Vik," I hurried to say. "At least not like that. I know you'll never hurt me. I know I'm physically safe with you."

A storm appeared in his gaze. "Physically. But not in other ways?"

Helpless, I floundered. My shoulders lifted in a shrug. "Vik, you could break my heart." My gaze dropped. Words cluttered my throat, thickening it. "After our kiss, I think it's pretty obvious that I care for you. Kissing always meant something different to you than it did to me. I don't want to go down this road if . . . if there's not something you feel as well."

Vik paused.

I closed my eyes, in agony. The courage it required to draw from my heart was a shallow spring.

Why so much silence?

Why didn't he *say* something?

Holy coconuts, but I'd laid myself out. Bare. Flayed open like bleeding love. All he had to do was look in my eyes to see the brimming adoration, the years of layered affection. He had to meet me halfway. He had to *do* or *say* something.

The clock ticked.

A car sped by outside.

When I gathered my courage to look up, Vik peered at me with a quizzical expression on his face. Bemusement. Terror. I couldn't tell the rotating emotions apart.

"Vik?" I murmured.

He shuffled closer. My head tilted back, breath caught, a second before his hand cupped my jaw and his lips found mine. He trapped me in a kiss that stole lifeblood. My spirit sparked. Soul sang. His other arm wrapped my back, fisted my shirt, and closed the gap between us.

I melted, held by his firm grip.

When he pulled away, blood raced past my ears. I stared at him, dazed. He studied me, cloudy with passion. The next words almost choked him. Only the pain in his gaze softened how difficult it was for him to say, "I care about you, too, Kate."

I reached up, touched his face. Though hardly a declaration of love or intent, I recognized the gesture for what it was—an attempt.

Vik tried.

He closed his eyes and leaned into my palm. Something happened between us. A click. A gentle shove forward. I sensed a slow crumbling inside him. A landslide not quite ready to break yet. Brave uncertainty compelled him forward in a way he had never done before. He moved slower than I might have liked, but this time Vik *moved*.

Progress.

I leaned against him, head to his chest. He held me there, heart pounding, until all the unease sluffed away.

"Give me time?" he pleaded.

My eyes closed. "Always," I whispered.

Chapter Twenty

VIKRAM

Not even fishing with Kate put me in a better mood.

The soothing tug of the line in my hands. Quiet *blips* of water in the lake. All of it moved past a serene backdrop that normally fed my soul. This time, I glowered in the canoe like a dark thunderstorm, a black hole of annoyance in the middle of a wild landscape.

We cuddled, dismissed the kiss and conversation thing without a word for the rest of the evening. Our words still floated through my mind all night, holding off sleep for too long. I woke cranky and sore and more frustrated than ever. One look at Kate's face as she handed me a mug of coffee this morning calmed the worst of it.

Kate.

Damn, but she could pull a punch. Force a guy to make a move—and wasn't that her right? If she didn't, would I move myself? Fifteen years indicated that no, I wouldn't. I'd lived and worked with men that could frighten a holy man, but none of them came at me with the truth like she did last night. No woman had ever denied such a benign advance.

I mean, cuddling?

Really, Kate?

With a breath, I dismissed my judgment of her. I wasn't being fair. She'd been open and honest last night, in ways I'd never gifted her. A niggling something in the back of my mind told me *that's* what she wanted. Honesty. Openness. Commitment.

Could I give it?

The question persisted.

The canoe rocked to the side as Kate shifted, readjusting so her legs crossed in front of her. She leaned back, a fishing pole tucked in the bend of her knee, arms trailing along the sides. Her fingertips created ripples in the unbroken glass of the water. Every now and then, she hummed. Like a sunsprite, she soaked up all the warmth and brought it to her dazzling, golden skin.

I looked away for the hundredth time.

No matter how much I admired her, *craved* her, I couldn't silence the voice in my head. The deeper one that floated free at the worst times. The one that promised pain with commitment. That reminded me only fools gave their power and focus and freedom away.

Then Hernandez, Bastian, and Grady are all fools, I thought.

The voice said nothing.

Pain, it promised. *Always pain.*

Where do you come from?

More silence, then Emma's face.

I sent her back with a scowl.

A dark horizon loomed ahead if the voice of fear proved to be true. If I couldn't trust Kate, then what woman could I trust? No one. Certainly no woman I had dated, that was clear. Other women hadn't been nearly as withholding or honest or fun or terrifying or agonizingly out of reach. Kate was a smooth cocktail, blended and shaken in all the right ways.

A soft gasp drew me out of my thoughts. Kate straightened with a snap. Her line tugged, sending tiny waves onto the water.

"I think I have one!"

"Easy," I said, reeling my own line in from the opposite side of the boat. "Just like we practiced. Give it a tug, then a little reel."

Her left hand gripped the pole while her right hand twirled the wheel. The line went taut with a little jerk, then began to pull in. Her line wavered back and forth as the fish struggled, resisting the pull. A glimmer of silver appeared near the canoe. She stopped.

Her astonished gaze lifted to mine.

"There's a fish on there!"

Laughing, I nodded. "Yes. That's why they call it fishing. Pull it in."

"But it will die."

"If you leave it out of the water too long, yes."

"I don't want it to die."

"Then you can release it."

Kate frowned at the water. The fish scuttled back and forth, frantic now. "Doesn't the lure hurt its lip?"

I shrugged. "I don't know how many nerves fish have. Better than dying, right?"

Unconvinced, she looked back in the water. Her brow wrinkled. "I don't want to touch it."

"I can help."

She lifted a hand. "No, I'll do it. It's my responsibility. I'm going to set it free."

With a little shudder, she handed off the fishing pole to me and reached into the water. I lifted the pole higher to bring the fish within reach. She spoke to it soothingly. A few grabby hands and squeals of disaster later, she had her fingers wrapped firmly around a small fish, not much longer than her palm.

Grimacing, Kate gently retracted the lure, then placed the

fish back in the water. It darted away, disappearing into murky depths. Once completed, she wrapped her arms around her knees. Her fingertips flicked fish scales free.

"Gross."

I laughed.

She fell into silence as I set her fishing pole to the side. When she turned to look at me again, she'd pulled the brim of her hat lower over her eyes.

"Why do you love fishing if you don't eat much meat?" she asked.

I shrugged. "Not sure. It's a reason to be outside, I think. I like meat, just in smaller doses than most people. If I'm going to eat an animal, I want to make sure it was fairly treated. Fishing trout from a mountain stream ensures that it lived a good life, I killed it humanely, and I don't waste it. Feels better that way."

Kate seemed to ponder that, then looked to the canyon walls again.

"Can I ask you a question?" I asked.

She leaned back again. Her hair swept back over her shoulders, looking warm and silky. The sun-warm strands would smell like wildflowers, I bet. I wanted to bury my fingers in it and pull her close.

"Sure."

"What's your favorite color?"

Her brow rose. "My favorite color?"

I nodded.

She bumbled with a reply, then stammered, "Um . . . purple, I think."

"Why?"

"Why is purple my favorite color?"

I rolled my lips to school back a laugh, charmed by her bewilderment. Her mouth lay slightly open, eyebrows crashed together.

"Yes. Why is purple your favorite?"

"I don't know." She tilted her head to the side. "I guess I've always thought the smell of lavender was soothing, and so was the gentle color. One time, Vini and I found a farm that grew lavender. You could walk through it and smell all the plants and learn about the growth cycle. It was really fun. We went there and had a good time. It was. . . . soothing."

"Huh."

She leaned forward, arms wrapped around bare knees. "You?"

"White."

"Really?"

I nodded.

"Why is white your favorite?"

"Reminds me of clouds and yoga and sunshine and a lot of things. Plus," I tacked on with a quick smile, "no one ever picks white. And why not? It softens every other color. It changes them in gentle ways and isn't as harsh as black."

A contemplative look crossed her face. "Fair," she murmured.

I tugged my line. Sensing nothing nearby, I pulled it in. The harried expression on Kate's face when she'd pulled her fish free —clearly, she couldn't stand any semblance of violence on a living thing—flashed through my mind. I tucked my lure under the bottom of my reel to hold it and slipped the pole into the canoe.

She eyed me as I sat back down, gripping both oars.

"What was your worst date?" I asked.

More on guard now that I'd pulled out one random question, she murmured, "I haven't been on one since before Timothy's attack."

My eyebrows rose. "Really?"

Her lips pressed into a thin line. Though sunglasses hid her eyes, I could tell she stared at me. Her eyes bore into mine when she nodded.

"Well," I murmured, "perhaps we should change that."

"Unless you count this." She swirled her hand to encompass the lake. "This is a pretty fun date. Fishing. Certainly outside the norm, which seems like that would be your thing."

I snorted, but it wasn't without amusement. "Thanks, I think. Do you want this to be a date?"

Kate swallowed. "Yeah," she whispered. "I do."

"Then a date it is. How do I compare?"

"To a pubescent sophomore who tried to cop a feel during a movie?" Her tone pitched higher in question, then dropped into a coy curl. "Definitely worse."

I splashed her with an oar.

She laughed.

The fragile ribbon of uncertainty that my curiosity inspired seemed to have disappeared, so I leaned into the now open air.

"What's your biggest dream?" I asked.

"Oh, ho," she murmured with a witty little smile. "Going for the big guns now, are we? This is just a first date, remember? Shouldn't you get to know me a little better before you start to ask the deep stuff?"

"To be fair," I countered, "I used to hang onto the superficial stuff on purpose. I avoided talk of real things because why do that? So, you can't thwart my attempt to be a better man here, Kate."

Though I said it with amusement, all levity dropped from her face. Her smile disappeared. She opened and then closed her mouth. An interminable silence later, she said softly, "I want to live without rules again. That's my biggest dream."

My eyebrows shot higher.

Whoa.

Wasn't expecting that.

Her hand waved through the air, as if to soften the suddenly deep and pervasive undertone around us.

"I mean, the rules protect me. They helped me through

what was a hard time but . . . now I kind of want to let them go. I just . . . I don't know how. In some ways, they were more than just rules. They were safety. Control. Yet, I think they've held me back now, I'm just not sure how. I'm not sure how to be safe without them."

I swallowed, utterly unable to speak.

Weren't we one and the same?

Didn't I live by my own set of rules meant to keep me safe? No commitment. No love. No pain.

She let out a sharp breath through her nose. "Talk about heavy," she muttered.

"No," I quickly said, "I like it. I'm just formulating a reply that doesn't make me sound like a selfish bastard."

"What do you mean?"

I pulled on the oars, buying myself a few more moments to scramble for the right words. What the hell was I doing? There were no *right* words. There were just words. She'd have to love them or hate them.

"Well, I say to hell with keeping yourself safe. Let me protect you."

Kate went totally still. Eventually, she straightened. I expected her to jump over the canoe, but she leaned closer.

"You say that, Vik, but . . ."

"I mean it."

"The implication has commitment written all over it. You spent your life declaring that your personality doesn't thrive in a committed world. You want freedom and openness and agency. While that happens in a relationship, it's not the same."

The barb struck right where it should—at the very heart center of my pain. I swallowed it, accepting the jab for what it was.

The truth.

"I know that such a statement implies commitment. I'm comfortable with that."

Kate tilted her chin a little higher. "Really?"

"The thought of losing you is more powerful than the other fears, and that's never happened before. You're not the only one that's afraid, Kate. Not the only one that is trying to venture into an unsafe world and do something new."

"Oh."

The sound was more surprise than understanding. Behind her dark glasses, I imagined her blinking. Could practically *hear* her thoughts from here. She wondered if I could be trusted, or if this was me attempting to win a conquest to prove something.

She put a piece of herself out there last night. I hoped she saw this as a reciprocal movement.

"You don't have to do anything with what I just admitted," I said quietly. "I only wanted you to know that I'm interested in something deeper than friendship between us, all right? I'm also going to suck at it," I added in a poor attempt at levity.

She snorted.

To have something to do, I continued pulling on the oars. The last thing I wanted was for her to feel trapped out on the lake with me, so I angled back toward land. The shore came into view at my back, not far from the Frolicking Moose. She'd be able to see her escape, at least.

Kate licked her lips and gazed away.

"Can I think about this?" she murmured quietly. "It feels . . . overwhelming. There's more that you don't . . ."

Her voice faded.

Relief washed through me. It wasn't a rebuttal or dismissal, at least. In truth, I wanted the time too.

With a nod I said, "Take all the time you need."

Chapter Twenty-One

KATELYN

Vini's voice screeched through the phone.

"He said what?"

I closed my eyes and groaned. "Don't make me repeat it again."

"You'd better!"

"Fine! He said, *the thought of losing you is more powerful than the other fears, and that's never happened before.*"

"Go Vik!" Vini cried. "That's the greatest line I have ever heard. Is it weird that I'm super proud of my brother?"

A small voice peeped out of me. "Me too."

"How are you feeling?" she hurried to ask. "After a line like that, I hope you feel like a bajillion bucks!"

"Scared, actually."

"Of Vik?"

"Of this falling apart." I sat up. Pillows cluttered my hips, tangled in blankets on top of my bed. Muted shadows lay on the house, and the distant sound of the air conditioner hummed in the background. My shorts bunched around the top of my thigh. I played with a few loose strings. "Vini, what would happen to me if Vik broke us up? What if he left? I'd lose my only family. You are all I have."

"You have to know that Amma and Appa would choose you over Vik."

I tilted my head back and laughed.

"C'mon, you know that's not true."

She giggled lightly. "It *is* true. Just because Vik's an idiot doesn't mean that we wouldn't make it work. We're family, Katelyn. You belong with us, whether or not Vik pulls his head of his—"

"What about family reunions?"

Her voice carried a shrug. "Can't be much different than the last ten years, right? Whenever Vik did show up, it was fine."

"It was hell," I muttered.

She paused. "Have you really loved him that long?"

My eyes closed, face clenched. "It sounds so pathetic," I whispered, splaying a hand over my eyes. "Really pathetic."

"It's super sweet! You could have the romance story of the century! Kate, this is epic, which means it would naturally be a little scary."

I swallowed, looking down the hall. His bedroom door, right next to mine, was open. A hint of lemongrass issued from inside. I suppressed the desire to climb back in his bed and wrap myself in his smell. If Vini knew we'd spooned through a thunderstorm, she'd press even harder on the little bravery I had left.

"Listen," Vini said on an exhale. "This is the most I've ever heard of Vik *trying*. He's actually attempting to be a normal human. You are the only person he's ever done that for and it means something. Vulnerability isn't his strong suit. Look at Appa, the man mistakes himself for a brick wall."

I chuckled. "True."

"If you're willing," Vini murmured, "let him know how you feel—have felt—and give him a little space and time to decide what to do with it. It's not fair for you to string yourself along when you can have an answer right now."

"What if he says no?"

"Then he's an idiot, he'll regret it, and you will move on with me at your side through every single moment. *The way you always have.*"

Tears sprang to my eyes. I swallowed them back. My voice was husky when I whispered, "I don't deserve you."

Vini snorted. "You absolutely deserve me. Can you do it, Kate?"

With a sniffle and a resolute nod, I firmly said, "Yes. I can do it. You're right. I need to tell him the whole truth."

"It might make him feel safer with you, you know? To know the depths of your feelings."

"Could scare him."

"It could," she murmured. "Knowing Vik? I don't think it will. The moment you finish talking to him, you call me. Better yet, call me, I'll mute, then put me on the table next to you on speakerphone so I can hear everything."

A laugh rolled out of me, softening the expectant, fractured tension.

"You want to eavesdrop on this very pivotal conversation with Vik?"

"You bet I do!"

"How about I call you right after?"

She blew a raspberry, then capitulated with exaggerated drama. "Fine. I'll deal with that."

I sobered with warm and tender love for her, my sister. "Thanks, Vini. Love you."

"Love you too—and talk soon!"

Once the call ended, I clutched my phone to my chest. My eyes closed on a long breath. Underneath it all lay a thrumming sense of courage. Vini was right—I needed to do this. Vikram showed signs of interest and wanting to move forward. Better to get it all aired out in the open.

He deserved it, too.

Thoughts of buying sushi popped into my head as I climbed off my bed to change. Sushi had always softened him up, put him in a good mood. He didn't always pack a lunch, either, so I could take it to him at work. Do it somewhere that wasn't here, where I could scuttle away to escape just in case.

A text message popped onto my screen as I yanked a pair of jeans on.

Bethany: Great news! I found the perfect little place for you to rent. It's in your price range, a five minute walk from the shop, and meets all your safety requirements. Want to go check it out later today?

My breath caught.

I shut my phone off, hesitated, then flipped it back on.

Kate: 3:00 all right?

Bethany: See you then.

Chapter Twenty-Two

VIKRAM

The Outfitters store held two main things: outdoor goods and time.

The thick timbers were aged, some of the bark peeling. Chinks in the outside had been covered with stain, some places reinforced. Inside, a modern-day air conditioner blasted cool air, and renovations led to a bright ambience. Still, the place smelled like bait and plastic and squeaky new shoes. The type of people that filtered through the store were my kind of people and the work was easy on my recovering leg.

In a word, the job was ideal.

"Oy, Vik!"

Daniel motioned to me from behind the counter, where he stood with a phone pressed to his ear. I stood in the back, near the stand-up paddle boards with a not-very-interested customer. A woman with blonde hair and a gaggle of children stood on the other side of the counter from Daniel. With a wave to acknowledge him, I checked with the browsing customer, then headed over.

My thoughts meandered briefly to Kate, who had still been asleep when I left for work at 9:00. I'd peeked into her room,

"

caught sight of tousled hair on a pillow, blankets tucked up around her shoulders. The urge to kiss her warm neck and snuggle in had haunted me ever since.

I had to stop *looking* at her.

But I couldn't.

My declaration of intent had sobered the air between us. Three times it looked as if Kate would say something significant, but never did. I went to bed, stewing over what it meant when she said *there's more* . . .

Whatever she had to say, I'd take it.

Kate was worth the work.

The woman at the counter poorly attempted to keep four children close by. A toddler pasted his slimy mouth against the glass display of GPS watches. Another one ducked under a rack of tourist t-shirts that said PINEVILLE: THE ONLY HOME YOU EVER NEED. The other two wailed, pinching each other in what looked like a near-bloody battle. The mother's hair was pulled away from her face, bedraggled. Old makeup smudged her eyes, and colored chapstick smeared the corners of her mouth.

She glanced up as I closed in with a bright smile. Two steps later, I froze. Her eyes widened. A breathy word escaped her thin lips.

"Vik?"

"Emma?"

Five seconds passed as we regarded each other, locked in a strange back-and-forth.

Was this real?

A shout from a nearby child drew her back to the moment. She clamped a firm hand on his shoulders, steered him into a corner, and ordered him to stand still. By the time she stormed back, spitting harsh commands, the spit-dripping toddler and the older one under the rack cowered on the floor at her feet.

She straightened again, breathless now.

Emma Goldmann in. the. flesh.

Time hadn't been kind to Emma Goldmann. The last I'd seen her had been graduation day, when we walked off a stage at different times, caught eyes across a crowd, and never saw each other again.

Fifteen years was too soon.

"Hey," I managed. I lifted my hands, then let them fall. "How are you?"

She cleared her throat, nudging the squirmy youngest with a foot and a dire glare. "Fine." A limp smile followed. "Just visiting my parents for the summer and came to get some tackle kits for the boys. They want to go fishing."

"Great. Yeah, we have those over here. I'll take you to them."

Cognizant of her following train, I waited until all the kids gained their feet to wind through the maze of racks, towers of shoes, and mountains of boxes toward a kids section at the back. The boys, sensing a future present, tagged along with a little more decorum.

A few minutes later, all four boys chattered like squirrels, comparing different packages in high-pitched voices. Emma stood awkwardly nearby, half her attention on them, the other half on not studying me too intently.

What did she see?

I saw a tired mother of four, a heartless girl who broke my heart while she attempted to destroy my reputation, and a woman that, for all intents and purposes, didn't seem happy. Did she presume I was a wash out who couldn't figure out a career path? A guy stuck in the small mountain town while working at the Outfitters?

Probably.

That seemed *partially* fair. Not the washout part, though.

"Those two are on sale." I pointed out a bright red pole in her eldest child's hands. "Just for today, though."

She didn't look at me.

"Great. Thanks."

The urge to bolt away threatened. With it, a morbid sense of embarrassment. When was the last time I had run away from any woman?

Fifteen years ago.

From this very Emma Goldmann.

She had wrenched out my heart and laughed at me in front of the whole school. After accepting my request to take her to prom, she showed up at the school with the baseball pitcher—practically high school royalty. While others looked on, she made fun of my tux, my partially stubbled chin, and the fact that I'd believed she would go with someone like me.

Every student in the room had laughed, or turned their back. Eye rolls, scoffs, derision followed for weeks.

That had been the last time I let a woman call the shots.

The last time I committed to liking a woman with my whole heart. The last time I let anyone inside far enough to matter. This tired mother of four—maybe more—had significantly altered the course of my life. Based on her furtive, almost-nervous glances, I had a feeling she knew it.

"Need anything else?" I asked brightly.

"No, thank you."

With a nod, and a blithe avoidance of eye contact, I slipped away. Back at the register, I hailed a new customer and tried to draw in a deep breath. The cacophony of Emma's kids descending into another wrath-fest rang through the room. Daniel rolled his eyes at the sound and disappeared into the back.

Seeing Emma after so many years didn't shake me. The quaking deep in my bones, the remembered betrayal from so long ago, had more to do with the sheer amount of time that spanned us. Time when I'd held onto Emma as a shining example of what women innately were—or could do.

The younger Emma.

As a fifteen-year-old freshman, I'd become an obsessive sycophant, a glutton for her attention. Crawled after her, did what she wanted, fawned over her presence. First date. First kiss. First of many things, and it had all been a joke. It culminated in the humiliation of prom.

The whole affair had been very high-school, quite dramatic, and caused a stir bigger than it should have. Emma spread lies about me, carried on the lips of other teenagers in the hallways for weeks. Laughs. Whispered rumors. Giggles from other girls. Some wouldn't even look at me after what she did. Every male knew she played with her food before devouring it.

I learned the hard way.

Grady had taken down two of the worst offenders to my pride, earning himself detention twice in two weeks. Hernandez had been more sneaky—he attacked gossiping football players off campus, the ones that tried to do the most damage to my name. Bastian growled his way into lunchroom conversations, shutting them down. In the months that followed, the Merry Idiots helped to salvage my pride.

Then I did the rest.

Playboy Vik rose to the spotlight, the lover of many. Flying lips, they said. My name became synonymous with conquest, not much else.

For years.

Like an open wound, a gap broke inside me. Emma Goldmann had moved on—into some unhappy, nondescript life that I should have seen coming for someone like her—yet I hadn't. After she was physically out of my life, I'd let her stay. Let her affect me in more ways than I deserved.

The truth slammed into me with centrifugal force: I kept her nasty business alive when it should have been dead long ago.

All this time, Emma lived and breathed in my thoughts, to what end?

We'd been children. She moved on. I held on. It marked

both of our lives. I breathed through the ugly truth, the pain, because now Kate stood in startling disparity to Emma in real life.

Did I want to keep proving Emma wrong?

Did I need to be the same asshole to others that she'd been to me?

No.

I never should have.

Burrowed beneath all those layers of pain that throbbed again, for the first time in how-many-years, came a quiet voice. A whisper of truth that I couldn't deny, even when faced with the nastiness of trauma.

There has never been another woman like Kate.

No matter how far I ran, how many women swooned, or how much fun I had across all experiences in life, I'd never felt what Kate stirred up in me now.

Never again, I promised myself. *Never again.*

A man came to the counter to buy wool hiking socks, and I croaked my way through the transaction. Emma ushered her kids toward the door, sent a discreet look to me out of the corner of her eye, and disappeared without a word. I had a feeling I knew why.

I would have done the same.

A voice to my right caused my painful heartbeats to squeeze to a stop, followed by the gentle touch of a hand on my arm.

"Vik?"

I turned to find Kate there, smiling. She wore a hat, her hair down underneath it. A pair of sunglasses perched on top of the brim reflected my startled, yet relieved, expression.

"Hey." She held up a bag. "I brought you lunch. If you have a minute, could we go talk outside?"

I yanked her in a long-armed, too-tight hug. She paused, clearly startled, then put her arms around my waist. When she squeezed, all the weird parts inside dissipated. There was no force more powerful than the sun.

Katelyn was *my* sun.

The bag crackled as she set it on the counter. I closed my eyes, breathing deep of her hair. Flowery shampoo, combined with . . . cotton. Dear heavens, did she throw our laundry in together again? I walked around for days, smelling parts of her on my shirt and almost dying every time. I sincerely hope she kept it up.

Her palms splayed across my back. She pulled away slightly, concern in her furrowed eyes.

"You okay, Vik?"

"Yep." I pushed away, hands on her shoulder. A smile surfaced to save me at the last second. "Just glad to see you."

"That's good to hear. I brought some sushi. Sounded good, and I know spicy is your favorite flavor. Can you take a lunch break, or have I missed it? Sorry if this is a problem, I just wanted to surprise you and . . . chat. You're always feeding me."

I put my hand on her arm and pulled her close. "Hey, Dan!" I called over her shoulder. "Going to lunch. Be back in thirty."

He waved from his desk, where he leaned so far back the chair threatened to tip. I swiped the bag and led her toward the door, relief unbraiding through my chest. I needed to get out of here, and I needed more of Kate.

"Let's eat outside."

* * *

A picnic table under a sprawling oak tree lay empty outside the store. Bird poop littered the far side, and the paint peeled in brown chunks off the edges of the board, but it would be a perfect escape from Emma. From inside.

From myself.

I set the bag of sushi down as Kate settled across from me.

She tilted her hat back. Her designer glasses were gone yet again, leaving her eyes as open oases. She wore my favorite pair of jeans and a bright yellow tank top. Most days, she fluttered around in simple summer dresses that exposed her tanned legs and strong ankles. They made me want to run my fingers around her knee while we watched movies together, carefully apart, but near.

The hell with that.

With Emma and all her memories kicked to the metaphorical curb, it was time to take this to the next level—after Kate said whatever she came to say. A gentle skein of silence passed while we set out our lunch. Kate kept chewing on her bottom lip, start-stopping, but never speaking.

"I just saw an old . . . acquaintance," I said to spare her whatever mental agony she might put herself through. Fear she was about to send me packing put a knot in my stomach. For all I knew, my advance yesterday would be rejected.

The *one* time it mattered.

She perked up, seeming relieved for a subject.

"Oh?"

She used a chopstick to separate a chunk of wasabi, then reached for a soy sauce packet. A California roll. The girl had always been so predictable.

Wait, no.

Not anymore. Kate surprised me every day, just not with her sushi order.

"Her name was Emma Goldmann, not sure if she's married or not at this point. She left the store just before you made yourself known."

Kate stiffened, then relaxed. "The name is familiar," she murmured. I popped the end of my roll inside my mouth and chewed. Soft and perfectly spicy, the hint of sriracha mayo a gentle bloom in my mouth.

"She was my first kiss."

Kate brightened. "Oh?"

I nodded, the story unraveling more easily than I expected. "Yeah, at fifteen, or something. We went on dates, hung out, that sort of thing. She called me her boyfriend, I did anything she wanted. I was totally enraptured with her and couldn't believe she'd give me the time of day."

Kate's chopsticks paused, stuck in the wasabi-soy mixture as she listened, mouth slightly open. "I vaguely remember her," she murmured, lashes lowering in thought. "Blonde hair?"

"Yep. Led the debate team, and controlled the whole school social ecosystem."

Kate snorted. "Mmm, yes. I definitely remember."

"Anyway, I asked her to prom, she said yes. Again, I couldn't believe it was true. She wasn't home when I showed up to get her. Her mother said she'd already left, which seemed weird."

"Uh oh," she murmured.

"Right," I drawled. "Uh oh. When I stepped into the school gymnasium, there she was. Wrapped in Tysin Montgomery's arms as they danced."

Kate blinked, eyes slightly tapered, as if she sorted through distant memories. "You confronted them, right?"

I nodded. She must remember the fallout at home.

It hadn't been pretty.

"Yeah, I did. Like a testosterone-driven idiot. Emma laughed at me, so did Tysin. In fact, the whole school laughed at me. I found out it had been a joke all along. They'd been spreading nasty rumors that weren't true, playing me. Her friends were in on it. The whole thing: a ruse."

Fire leapt into Kate's eyes. A gratifying, righteous anger that made me want to laugh. Set against the backdrop of Emma's easy cruelty, the two couldn't be more different. One, an avenging angel. The other a fallen star.

"Your parents got involved, right?" Kate asked haltingly, riding the edge of a memory. With my own chopsticks, I separated another piece of the sushi roll and nodded. Each word sent the pain farther away, like blowing out all the smoke to leave clean air again.

"Yes. The principal, Emma's parents, it was a huge fiasco. School was a nightmare for weeks. Kids making fun of me, outright ignoring me. I lost all my other friends except the Merry Idiots, all my presence in the world. Maybe it sounds a little stupid now," I said dismissively, "but at the time I was devastated."

Her eyes widened. "Then what happened?"

"Grady took matters into his own hands."

"Grady?"

"Yeah. He used those big hands of his and took on the worst of the guys that kept spreading rumors. They tried to rough me up a few times after school, but Hernandez tackled them. Bastian had my back in the halls, so they were only scuffles. For a while, though, I couldn't walk anywhere alone."

"Were the other boys jealous or something?"

He shrugged. "They claimed they were protecting her from me. The rumors she spread ballooned as they were tossed around. Some kids tried to say I'd hit her once, which absolutely *wasn't* true."

"Wow."

"My boys had my back."

A tilt of her lips revealed real warmth. "Oh, the Merry Idiots," she murmured. "The four of you were quite the crew."

I flashed a quick smile, chewing through another bite. "After Emma's betrayal?" I shrugged. "I just . . . it all changed."

"Dating, you mean?"

"Life."

"Is that when you became . . . ahh . . ."

Heat flooded her cheeks. I lifted my brow in teasing interest. "Please," I murmured, "do finish that statement."

A twinkling overtook her embarrassment. "Loose Vik with Flying Lips?"

The old nickname sent me into a spasm of amusement, and then a stab of regret. How stupid it sounded now.

"Yes," I drawled. "I flipped the metaphorical bird to women, so to speak. Part of the reason we became the Merry Idiots, known for the C-tape, was probably an attempt for me to recover some footing. Stable ground. A . . . name for myself that had nothing to do with Emma and her games."

"I remember."

She said it so softly, I almost didn't hear.

With a quiet breath, I exclaimed, "Damn, it all seems so stupid now." A hesitant, embarrassed smile came next. "At the time, though, it was . . . so hard."

"Retrospect is easy."

I shrugged. "Yes, but here's the really dumb part: I haven't forgotten Emma."

"Who would?"

"No, I mean I've let her haunt me all through my adulthood. That period of my life has had . . . all this impact." I spread my hands, frustrated with the truth of it. "Seeing her today forced me to realize how stupid I've been."

She paused halfway through a bite of sushi, washed it down with a drink of water, and tilted her head.

"Now? You just realized it now?"

"Yes." I laughed. The whole thing was out now, so I leaned into it. "Isn't that wild? Emma walks into the store, we have the most awkward reunion ever, and she hurries out as quickly as she can. She has at least four kids, looks totally miserable, and could barely make eye contact with me. Then my brain sort of explodes when I realize I've been angry at her all this time and taking it out on women by being a serial dater. Picking them up and putting them down as heartlessly as she did to me."

Kate blinked, her thick lashes hiding churning thoughts. Quiet rolled between us, burdened with all I'd just said. The unbuttoning of the past left me feeling more open than I had in years.

Clarity had such power.

"Those days are over," I said when it all became too much. The verge of something glimmered on my horizon now. A welling energy bubbled up, fraught with power and excitement and something I couldn't quite put my finger on.

I set my elbows on the table, hands steepled in front of me. Questions layered her wide eyes. I imagined if I pulled each back, one at a time, I'd never get to the bottom of Kate.

A breathless question came from her. "What does that mean?"

"It means . . ."

My reply stalled as I lost myself in her gaze. How honest could I be right now? Emma stirred up ideas and thoughts that swirled around Kate and lost opportunities and seizing the moment for the first time in my life. Would I frighten Kate if I told her what I *really* wanted to say?

Probably.

But that wouldn't stop me.

I leaned forward. "When I saw Emma, I figured out what she never made me feel, even at the height of my obsession with her. With Emma, I never felt happy. I know that because it's how I feel when I'm around you. Kate, you make me want to be better. You make me want to stay. You make me want to forget Emma and be a better Vik. Kate, I love you."

Chapter Twenty-Three

KATELYN

Shock hit me like glacier towers.

Hard concrete.

Immobility.

Total suspension in time.

My breath caught in the back of my throat, suspended there. I couldn't move. Didn't breathe. Wasn't entirely sure that what I'd just experienced was real. Had Vikram *really* just laid himself bare?

Vikram?

Before I'd even given him the safety of doing so. Vikram had just taken a massive leap of emotional faith.

Right into me.

His intent gaze, locked on me, stabilized the seconds that followed his declaration. I swallowed, licked my lips.

Did he just say . .

No.

He couldn't have.

Yet I didn't imagine it. Did I? Was this one of those dreams that tortured me all the time? The ones where my ideal story played out, whispering across the landscape with surreal beauty, until the dream left me behind in the morning?

A pinch confirmed that I hadn't imagined it.

"I'm sorry," I whispered. "What?"

Amusement and fear appeared in a quick smile at the same time. He leaned closer, his hand dropping on top of mine.

"Kate, I'm crazy about you. I wanted you to know because . . . dancing around it seems so silly. We've lived together for months and I've been fighting it and I can't anymore. Emma made me realize that none of what I felt for her or anyone else was real. What I feel around you *is* real. I love you."

The textured shadows of his hand, so heavy on mine, felt like an anchoring weight. A musky smell drifted off him, making it impossible to breathe without the smell of Vikram twined throughout.

Everything swirled around, tightening my chest, until a gentle finger on my chin jerked me free. Vikram tilted my head back, peering into my eyes.

"Kate?"

"Yes?"

"It's okay, whatever you say."

Tears welled up. Disbelief burst through all the questions, all the barriers to tackle. After it, a heady euphoria followed. Sweet baby pineapple, but he'd just said the words I'd waited to hear *all my life*. The little girl's dreams that carried me through the darkness of my aunt's house played out with starting clarity.

My lips rolled together. He'd given me honesty, and I yearned to do the same. No matter how frightening.

"Vik, I've loved you since I was ten."

This time, *his* eyes widened. An astonished pause, and then a raspy, "What?"

A giggle escaped me at our interchanging reactions. Would we always surprise each other?

"Ten," I whispered.

"That's when you moved into your aunt's house next door."

Another nod.

Vik leaned back, which broke our hands apart. The space gave me room to breathe, but I monitored him carefully. Would this freak him out in return? Such honesty would certainly test his resolve. If he really meant what he'd said, my truth should delight him.

"That first day I moved in? I met you first, then Vini. Vini and I became inseparable friends and I loved you from the sidelines all my life."

The sushi lay abandoned between us as I rubbed my sweaty palms along my jeans, eager to get this out. Now that the knot had uncoiled, I wanted it to whip free. Flap around.

Reveal it all.

Not even the crystalline vulnerability of revealing myself so openly could frighten me now. Freedom. He'd offered me a chance to unload the truth and stop hiding.

"I was sort of pathetic about it," I said through a miserly laugh, ignoring his dazed expression. A glazed look swept over his face, as if he sorted back through the memories with a magnifying glass.

"You were so shy around me," he murmured. "Is that why?"

"Partly. A lot of my reticence had to do with my aunt and the environment she raised me in. Mostly, though? My crush on you. It developed over the years, growing every single day. Sometimes it felt like a thing inside me that I couldn't control."

Vik blinked his sooty lashes.

"If that's truly how you felt, I wanted you to know everything. The truth, I suppose. Vini knows how I feel about you, but only recently. Your parents have no idea, as far as I can tell."

"Is this an in-the-past kind of thing?"

My heart quivered. "No," I whispered.

He frowned. "Is that why you hesitated to move in with me?"

I nodded, then chuckled softly. "Seemed like a special way to torture myself. Surrounding myself with you when I couldn't have you? Torture."

"Has it been?"

"The best kind," I murmured.

Vik dragged his hand through his hair, shunting the strands away from his face. I could barely stand to look at him. An ache deep in my chest resonated powerfully. His lithe beauty. His protection.

Had I just lost it all?

Didn't matter. Having it out felt too good.

"I . . . I'm not sure what I want to say," he murmured. "Just that, damn. I'm such a lucky guy."

My head lifted, shocked.

"What?"

A bright, elated smile crossed his face. He laughed, head tilted back. My stomach curled. Would there ever be a time when I didn't ogle him? Sink into the reverie that was Vikram? In a second, he shot off the bench and at my side. He pulled me from the table and into his arms. My heart banged against his ribcage, taking flight. The dazed feeling of this not being real followed as I looped my arms around him. He felt firm and solid.

Me.

In Vikram's arms.

Like some astonishing, elaborate Cinderella story.

He reached up, a hand touching my face. The edge of my jaw, the top of my collarbone. His fingertips moved like a whisper until they dropped to my hips, holding me there.

"Kate," he murmured. "You're too good to be true."

"Is this real?" I whispered.

"I hope so."

"Do you care about me like that? Not just as a sister, but as more?"

Not a breath of hesitation lingered between the question and his response.

"Yes."

"Can we do this?"

Another laugh, a flashing grin. He pulled me closer. "Not only can we," he whispered, "but we *will*."

My eyes dropped to his lips, then back. A smoldering heat built there, but he didn't move. The sense of waiting slowed time, stalled sound. A bubble formed where we hovered, caught in the in-between.

I never wanted it to break.

I lifted my hand to his face and pulled his lips to mine. He came willingly, gently, with the supple press of warmth. A shiver rocketed through me, puckering the skin over my arms. A growl from him and he slanted to the side, deepening the kiss.

I fell into it.

Into Vikram.

The love of my life.

* * *

Stars whirled over my head that afternoon.

In the quiet, cool air of the living room, I lay across the couch and clutched a pillow to my chest. For the tenth time, I replayed what had just happened outside the Outfitters store.

Vikram.

Kiss.

Ohmygoshwhatjusthappened.

The shock ran through me in waves. Gradually, at first, then in greater, spreading ripples that I couldn't justify away. This hadn't been a dream. Vikram really *cared* about me, just like Vini said.

She'd never let us forget it, either.

A giddy laugh bubbled out of me, like a lovestruck high-school girl whose dreams had just come true. Wasn't that perfect, though? It's exactly what happened. The frightened, teenage Kate inside just received her heart's desire.

The kiss replayed back through my lips in a wave of heat. The play of his hands on my body. He sat next to me while we ate, both of us contemplative. His hands didn't leave me the whole time. Always on my skin, my body. The tenderness of his touch sent a cascade of warmth through me now.

For the tenth time, I looked at the clock.

Two more hours.

The urge to be near him, to reaffirm what we'd spoken over stolen time at lunch, agitated me. Too soon after the declarations had been made, Vikram had to return to work. The sushi had been cleared away, a lingering kiss exchanged, tepid, but sincere. The distance to think was welcome but also loathed.

Soon, I'd want confirmation. The whole day felt like racing fire. A match lit, the blaze begun.

No going back.

With a muttered swear word, I shoved off the couch and stalked to the closet, where the vacuum awaited. An interminable two hours to kill before he returned home. I could call Vini and tell her everything—she'd exclaim over it the whole two hours if I let her—but I wouldn't. This fledgling, precious thing belonged to me and Vik for now. A fragile bubble to hold, extended between our hearts, until we had truly figured it out.

History lay in between us like a bulkhead, and I needed to understand what it meant that he cared now. That I cared ever since we'd met. Did such a thing build us together stronger, or work against us? We flowed together in life so easily, it was like twirling stars. I couldn't imagine our power fading.

With a bolt of inspiration, I reached for my car keys and my phone. A quick text message to Bethany accompanied me out the door.

Katelyn: Thanks for the help! I don't think I'll need the showing anymore :)

With two hours left, I knew exactly how to kill the time.

* * *

My retreat to Tempest Lake was intentional.

Azure skies swept me there. Fluffy clouds. Twittering birds. The gentle hum of the mountains, which was really no sound at all. Gravel ground beneath my shoe as I stepped into the parking lot, drew in a deep breath, and cast my gaze around.

No one else.

A prickle deep in my chest warned me that rules existed for a reason. Blatantly ignoring them out of sheer euphoria was foolish, at best. Years of structure couldn't just be erased, they told me.

You're right, I said. *But there is also life to live, and safety to create away from hiding.*

My hand went to my pocket, where I still carried my can of pepper spray. My phone lay in my other hand.

I had this.

I ignored their apprehensive cries.

With a backpack full of snacks, water, a change of clothes, and a towel, I set onto the trail. Bushes and trees trapped the heat in a lush stretch as I wound through the forest. Without Vikram to share my exclamations, the still-wondrous experience rang empty. The rough brown mushrooms. Deer prints. Sticks that formed an arrow pointing down the trail, no doubt set there by some clever hiker.

Fun.

But not fantastic.

The sunshine left a persuasive kiss on my skin as I approached the lake. At the edge, I stopped, closed my eyes, and pulled in a deep breath. For years I'd been by myself at times, but never wild. Weeks sometimes passed where I hid away from the world, attempting to recover my courage.

Today, fears didn't accompany my solo jaunt into the world. They didn't follow me here. What Timothy did to me had been a violent tragedy, but it wasn't the sum of me. Though I'd long ago reconciled to the fact that it wasn't my fault he attacked me, the truth hadn't really settled until now.

Even the most powerful rules couldn't stop bad things from happening.

The realization settled deep into my soul. Whether or not I liked it didn't matter. I could let the rules go simply by holding to wisdom and trusting myself. Today, at Tempest Lake, I would prove that.

"Thank you," I murmured, mentally picturing the list of rules in my head. "Thank you for helping me feel safe, for protecting me when I needed it. Now, I'm ready for something more. There is wisdom in safety and structure, and I won't release all my caution, but I will loosen my grip. I need room to grow, to experience life, and to do so wisely. Thank you for bringing me this far."

No response stirred.

The natural world continued on in unimpeded silence, but something settled in my chest. Quiet, like a door closing.

A road ending.

A new trail beginning.

Lakeside now, I slipped my hiking shoes off, carried them in my arm, and picked my way along the edge. Trees ringed Tempest Lake, which had a perimeter that undulated in ribbon-like waves. Sometimes I could see parts of the bank, others were hidden in twists and turns, and other times I couldn't. A cove existed not far from here, out of sight for hikers passing through. It lay in sunshine, where the water would be warm.

My thoughts meandered, unburdened in a way I hadn't experienced . . . maybe ever . . . when a rustle came from ahead. I tensed, looked up, and gasped.

Timothy peered at me from the trees.

Chapter Twenty-Four

VIKRAM

The day dragged into eternity.

From the moment Kate left, minutes became hours. I eyed the clock, attempted to stay busy, and tried not to bother Daniel in his office. The desire to be with Kate again compelled me home.

I just wanted to *hold* her.

On my last break, an hour before I could go home, my phone buzzed in my pocket. Grady. The quiet store lay open around me, so I stepped behind the counter to answer.

"Grady," I drawled. "Hey brother. Long time, no talk."

Grady laughed, a baritone roll of thunder in my ear.

"What's up, Vik?"

"Not much right now, how are you, man?"

"Rocking and rolling over here. Married life is the best. And don't try to play stupid with me. I heard you almost went septic after a knee surgery and didn't tell anyone."

"Hernandez needs to shut his big mouth."

His amusement deepened into another laugh at my expense. "Bastian mentioned it too, for what it's worth. Apparently, he gets all the gossip about you from your new girl."

Now *that* had my interest.

"Oh yeah? What did she say?"

"Naw, man. I'm not going to make it that easy." Grady tsked. "You gotta work for the info if you want it! Tell me who she is, first. Any girl that you've flipped for is a girl worth knowing. Hernandez said you're mooning over her."

I grinned. He wasn't wrong.

"It's Kate. You remember her?"

His voice pitched here. "Vini's friend?"

"The one."

"Quiet little Kate?" he cried.

"Not so quiet anymore. She's totally different now. Life had a way of . . . forcing her to grow up. She's pretty bold. Fearless. Very brave. I'm super proud of who she's become."

A pause, then he chuckled. "I never would have seen that one coming, but now that you say it, it fits. She's cute and she'll tolerate you, which is something we haven't seen together in awhile."

"You're the worst."

Grady hooted.

I shook my head. "It's stupid, but you're right. Too right. Kate's the best thing that ever happened to me."

"Big words for you, my man."

"They're true."

Grady whirled, low. "Hernandez is right. You've got it bad. C'mon, admit it. You should have seen this sooner."

"Shut up."

He hooted. His amusement at my expense today was far from comical, even though he hadn't stopped laughing.

"Guess who I saw?" I asked, before he could extrapolate further on my faults as a man. Grady loved poking at us, and only Bastian with those long arms and big shoulders really had a prayer of holding against Grady's huge hands when it came to a brawl.

"Who?"

"Emma Goldmann."

His voice lilted in shock. "That hag is still around Pineville?"

"Apparently."

His hilarity faded into surprise as I gave him a high-level view of what happened. I ended it with, "Kate brought me sushi for lunch right after Emma left, and I realized that Emma's a friggin' mess. I held onto her too long, so . . ."

"You made a move on Kate?"

"Don't gross it up," I muttered. "I told Kate how I felt. Turns out she's in love with me and has been for awhile."

"There's that big ol' F-word," Grady murmured, sounding just like his father. "Feelings. Sounds like you're a thing?"

"Damn straight."

"You're dating?"

"Yes."

"Just her?"

"Yes!" I cried.

"So you're a couple."

"Is this high school?" I cried. "What the hell, Grady? Yes, we're dating. We're a couple. I will not look at, touch, or discuss other women. Can we move on now? This is not a cataclysmic event."

"False," he countered. "You're committed to a woman and you used the feelings word with her. I dunno, Vik. Sounds like you've gone and caught yourself a relationship. Have you set yourself on fire yet?"

I rolled my eyes. The teasing I had expected. "No, but she does," I added in a mumble.

Grady howled. "He's gone," he called, whistling low again. "The boy is gone, ladies and gentlemen. Vikram has exited the single building, and just found his way to the next step. Someone give the damn man a flashlight."

"What did you call for, Grady?"

"This!" He laughed, a belly-deep sound that made my lips twitch—despite myself. "Hernandez told me that a committed relationship was inevitable for you, and I didn't believe it. I was wrong." He hooted. "I was *so* wrong. Vik, I can't wait to see her again, man. This is gold."

Despite myself, I laughed.

"Glad you're entertained at my expense."

Grady's hilarity sobered. "It's not just that, Vik, and you know it. I'm happy for you, right? These girls, man. They change who we are." I pictured his long fingers curling into a fist that he set against his chest. "We're better men because of them. Without them? We're nothing."

How deeply I knew that.

"I feel you, brother." My phone clicked. I glanced down to see Kate's name on the screen. "Gotta go, all right? Kate's calling."

"Get her, my friend. Oh, and don't mess this one up with your head, all right? Kate has always been a keeper."

"That much I can promise."

The phone switched over to Kate's call when Grady hung up. I swiped up to answer.

"Hey!"

A frantic voice came from the other side, hazy and distorted. "Vik?"

I perked up, dread pooling in my belly.

"Kate? What's wrong?"

"Tempest . . . Timothy . . . come right now."

Chapter Twenty-Five

KATELYN

With Timothy's beady glare on me, my hand immediately dropped to my front pocket, where the trusty can of pepper spray waited. Timothy tensed. His gaze dropped to my hand, back to my face. He leaned back, legs braced.

All the self-defense classes I completed every year stood to attention in my mind. I squared my shoulders, fingers tight around the canister. The situation came from muscle memory now. Had I spent years preparing for this moment?

Yes.

Now?

I was ready.

"Stay back," I commanded.

Timothy held up both hands. "I have no intention of hurting anyone today."

My throat thickened. *Did you intend to hurt someone then?* I almost asked. *Did you plan out such desecration?*

With shaking hands, I dropped my backpack, kept my gaze on him, and crouched next to it. Timothy eyed me as I reached for my phone. Seeing it, he lunged forward.

"Wait!"

"No!"

My shout stirred a nearby flock of birds. They rose from the trees, protesting with obnoxious squawks. Timothy skittered back, nearly tripping over a rock in his haste to move away. His nostrils flared as he regarded me.

"Don't call anyone."

I ignored him, but felt the vibrant fear in his voice. The phone brightened, activating with a quick touch. To avoid taking my eyes off Timothy to dial, I commanded, "Call Vikram."

By some miracle of technology, the command went through. Seconds later, a ringing phone broke the air. Spray pointed at Timothy, I kept a wary eye on him. He shuffled back another step.

"Hey," Vik said.

"I'm at Tempest Lake," I blurt out. "Timothy is here. I need you to come right now."

A pause for less than a breath followed.

"I'm . . . way."

The call cut out.

Relief swelled through me. If he cut through Daniel's private land—which I had no doubt he would do—Vikram could be at the trailhead in fifteen minutes. I could handle this for that long.

Timothy lifted one hand in the air, as if that would fend me off.

"I don't want to ever talk to you again," he muttered. "I didn't follow you. I'm just . . . here for a little time."

Behind him, hints of a rough camp were just visible. An old tent. Draped bags that looked like water purifiers. A sleeping bag hung over branches.

"Is this what you were stealing from garages?" I asked.

His nostrils flared. "Sometimes."

"What did you sell behind the coffee shop?"

A twisted expression crossed his face before he muttered, "All the rest. I have to eat somehow."

"So you stole things and sold them?"

He shrugged.

My feet twitched to step away from him, to head back to the parking lot, but I couldn't do that without turning my back. If I attempted to walk backward while keeping my eyes on him, I could trip over something and land in the water. It would be just the moment Timothy needed to do something drastic and stupid.

Never. Again.

Timothy's nose twitched as I gazed around, then back to him. He hadn't moved, frozen in position. Yet again, I had startled him as much as he startled me. I kept the phone in my hand, a wary eye on Timothy. He backed up one step, nostrils flared. It looked more like he braced himself than attempted to leave. He shoved a hand over his head, teeth clenched.

"How about we both leave at the same time?" I suggested.

"Was that your boyfriend?"

"Yes."

"Vikram?" His nostrils flared. "He'll call Hernandez."

I swallowed.

"Damn you, Kate! Now the deputies will come and my cover is blown."

I edged backward. Memories threatened to surface, but I wouldn't let them. I covered their simmering, hot forms and forced myself to think. This time, I wasn't without advantage. Help was on the way. I had pepper spray to at least blind Timothy until I could get away. Daylight. Awareness. Years of classes to help me defend myself. This wasn't the same Kate he took advantage of before.

Carefully, I shuffled a step back. A twig cracked under my weight.

"Let's take this easy," I murmured. "I'll head back to my car, you stay here. Vikram will take me away as soon as he arrives."

"No!" he screamed. "No! That is not how this is going to work! I can't go back there, Kate. I won't go back to jail!"

Roosted birds on the other side of the lake took to the sky, skittering off. He paced back and forth in a tight line, his muscles coiled agitation. He muttered, grunting, growling to himself.

"You can still get away!" I cried. "Look! You have the whole forest. Just pack up your camp and go. You have time. Vikram lost reception. I wouldn't even be able to tell Hernandez until I get back to Pineville, and I won't do it if you just let me go. You could be long gone."

Rage contorted his features.

Wrong thing to say. A lie, all of it. I'd tell Hernandez the *moment* I returned, but all that mattered was escaping.

I slipped back another step. My left foot dropped down an embankment in a fall of dirt, so I scuttled to the right. Another four steps gave greater distance. His head jerked up. He saw me farther back and scowled. His features contorted into a dark growl.

"Oh, no. Not so easy this time. There's nowhere for me to go, and nothing for me to do here. You don't get to keep living your happy life while I flounder in jail. I can't move because I don't have any money and my parents died while I was in jail. How do you like that? You put me there, and now I have nothing."

In a flash, my fear turned to wrath. An irate indignation bubbled inside, fueled by the scorn I felt all the way to my bones. I stopped scrambling back.

"You did it to yourself."

He stopped. "What?"

"You put yourself in jail when you raped me," I hissed. "You chose the path that your life is on now. You took something from me that wasn't yours to have and now you're paying for it. You don't get to blame this on *me*."

The words thickened my throat, but I forced them out. Finally, the chance to say what I had always wanted to say. To release the vitriol that swelled up in my body day after day after day. The ramifications of his choices had rippled into *my* life, and now he would know that.

"You chose your path, Timothy," I thundered. "And now you're on it. You cannot blame that on me. I was and am innocent."

Tears flooded my eyes. Furiously, I blinked them back. He gaped, mouth open, eyes narrowed, like a confused ox. Another three steps carried me farther away from him. The shock faded from his eyes.

He charged.

In the space of a breath, I comprehended that the moment had finally come. As Kinoshi had warned me, Timothy found himself in desperate circumstances that he blamed me for. Now, he'd thrown all caution to the wind in yet another rash decision that would decide the rest of his life.

This time, I wasn't going down with him.

I had less than five seconds to choose my *own* path. Running into the water would only give him the opportunity to more easily drown me. Though I excelled at swimming, his broader shoulders would carry him faster. I couldn't fight him in the water. Dodging through the undergrowth would be too slow. One trip and I'd be done. He'd pounce on me and—

Never. Again.

With an indrawn breath I braced my legs, squared my shoulders, and waited.

Time slowed as he neared. Every contorted muscle in his face, the tension in his shoulders, the reddened skin, played out in front of me. The night of his first attack had been dark. Rainy. Thunderous. Despite so many years passing, I struggled to make sense of the sequence of events. For such a life-altering event, it had been over more quickly than I must have expected.

Minutes, and the world changed.

Now, I stood under an open, brilliant sky. Light suffused the world. No sound accompanied his rush at me. With my chin held high, and the bull barreling at me, I waited.

This time, I was ready.

Seconds, and the world changed.

A breath before he reached me, I let the pepper spray loose. The stringy liquid found its mark. He howled, jerked back, and clawed at his face. Water sprang to my eyes from the thick, terrible scent as it filled the air. Timothy screamed, scrambling in the grass as he dropped to his knees.

I darted to the side, away from the cloudy haze.

He flung an arm out, hand clamping around my ankle. I tripped, landing in the grass with a thud. Breath whooshed out of me. For one terrible moment, I saw Timothy poised above, large and animalistic and terrible.

Never. Again.

I lashed out with a cry. My fingernails raked his face. He screamed, but didn't dodge away. With my right leg, I kicked up. My heel connected with his throat. A crunch followed.

Timothy toppled.

He dropped to his hands and knees with a high-pitched scream, then a wheezy sound. I scrambled to my hands and knees. When he canted my way, I delivered the hardest heel kick to his groin I could muster.

"I hope you rot in prison," I growled.

He toppled to the ground.

* * *

I rushed into the trees. Bushes, branches, trees tore at my hands. In my bare feet, I raced over roots and logs. My heart slammed in my chest as I sprinted away. Every ten steps, I looked back.

No sign of Timothy.

Eventually, I stumbled onto a trail that looped all the way around Tempest Lake. How many minutes had passed? How soon until Vikram arrived? A quick glance over my shoulder confirmed Timothy still didn't follow. Unlikely, after a kick to the groin that intense.

Tears streamed down my face from the spray while I ran. My chest burned. I wanted to throw up, but I pressed harder instead. The trail, the lake, the trees, sailed past me until I rounded a bend that took me to the top of the lake, where I first stepped off the trail that led to here. My car would be half a mile away.

A body skidded into view.

With a strangled cry, I waved my hand. "Vik!"

Vik whirled, saw me, and darted over. I closed the distance between us with a sob, throwing myself into his chest. He caught me, arms wrapped around me like cement blocks. Relief and terror filled his voice.

"Kate!"

A nonsensical blur of words streamed out of me as I tried to claw him closer. He whispered soothing sounds that I barely heard.

"Tim . . . lake . . . back there . . ."

Vik pulled away, put his hands on my cheeks, and forced me to look into his eyes. My fingertips began to tingle. The air felt thin and strained, my chest too heavy to pull in a breath.

Darkness encroached from the edges.

"I've got you, lady. You're safe." He put a hand on my chest. The warm, reassuring weight made it real.

Vik was here.

"In," he commanded.

A shuddering breath followed.

"Hold."

I paused, my eyes holding his.

"Out."

My chest began to loosen as I let it whoosh free, making way for a rush of warm air. The reprieve filled my lungs, whipped through my body. The lightheaded feeling began to fade. He pulled me back into him, firm around my back. I pressed my cheek to his chest.

When my breathing slowed, when the panicked, desperate gasps faded, Vik put his hands on my shoulders and studied me. Tears tracked down my face. My eyes stung, as if I'd stayed awake for too long.

Rage hardened his voice.

"Did he touch you?"

I shook my head and held out a trembling hand. Vik sniffed, glanced down the pepper spray in my shaking palm.

"I sprayed him," I whispered, "but he still reached for me, so I kicked him in the throat."

His eyes widened in a mixture of concern and delight.

"Really?"

I sniffled. "He was still coming at me, so I nailed him in balls while he was down. After that, I ran."

He regarded me, then let out a relieved laugh. He pulled me back into his hold and pressed a kiss to the top of my head.

"Sweet baby pineapple, as you would say," he muttered, "you're one hell of a woman, Kate."

"Thank you."

His fingers combed the hair out of my face. "Always, Kate. Always. I will always come for you, always protect you. Sounds like you don't need me, though. You protected yourself just fine."

Yes, I did.

"No," I murmured, tucking myself back into his arms. "I will always let you protect me."

The chatter of a radio broke behind us. Arms still around me, Vik canted to the side, calling over his shoulder.

"Hernandez, over here."

Hernandez stepped into view, brow drawn low in professional concern. He strode over, boots a dull thud on the trail.

"Where is he?"

"Down the trail," I whispered. "On the left, he has a camp on the edge of the lake. He's . . . laying in the grass."

"What?"

"She sprayed him, kicked him in the throat, and then the balls."

Hernandez chuckled. "Niiiice," he drawled. "Girl gets her justice. No worries, you two. I got this. Meet me back in the parking lot so I can hear your side of things, all right?"

He swept past, speaking into his radio.

Vik tightened his hold on me. He pressed a kiss to my temple. "C'mon. Today, you are the Kingslayer. Let's head back to the car. Hernandez said he'd call for backup on his way here. We can get this all over with for you, then go home. With me," he added. "Where you will always belong."

Chapter Twenty-Six

VIKRAM

Twirling lights, an ambulance, several police cars, and a gaggle of people later, I led Kate to the passenger door of the Jeep.

She leaned into me as she walked, a bit dazed. Sometime in the interim, Hernandez had returned with her backpack, which I carried on my shoulder. In the past hour-and-a-half, I hadn't let go of her. She pasted herself to my side, close as breath.

Somewhere back in the tangle of police cars and EMT's, Hernandez dismissed the ambulance with a slap on the side. They pulled away from the gravel turn-off without sirens, whisking the bastard away. Timothy lay on a gurney with a bruised trachea, chemical burns on his face from the pepper spray, and an ice pack on his crotch.

A lifetime of regret awaited him.

As deputies dispersed, and Kate's questioning finalized, the adrenaline had subsided. Her knees didn't knock together anymore, nor did her voice rattle. The shock bleached into disbelief, then a deep-seated relief.

Closure.

Power.

Kate could live free again. She'd been given the rare opportunity to stand against her assaulter and come out king.

The Eternal Second advanced to Kingslayer.

She always had it in her.

I tightened my hold on her shoulders. When she tipped her head closer, I pressed a kiss to the top again.

"Let's get you home," I murmured.

Later, we'd return for her car. She stopped at the door of the Jeep and turned to face me. I paused in silent question, fingers wrapped around the handle. She set a hand on my chest. Her warm fingers stirred my gut.

"Thank you," she murmured.

I put a hand over hers, fingers tightening.

"I will always protect you, Kate. Always."

"Same, Vikram." Her fingers pressed more firmly into my chest, right over the *thud-thud-thud* of my heart. "What if we protect each other?"

"What are you trying to say?"

"Mind if I stay at your place? Bethany found another one, but . . ."

I gently pressed her back to the door, braced my hands on either side of her head. "You're asking the wrong question," I growled.

Amusement flickered through her eyes as she smiled at me. "Oh?"

"The question is *will I ever let you go*? And the answer is *not while I have breath*."

Tears welled up in her eyes as I met her in a dizzying kiss. The tender touch grounded both of us. A reminder. A promise. Her pliable lips softened, opened to me, and filled me with warmth.

With love.

This is what I had been missing all along.

Kate.
The sun in my sky.
My Eternal Kingslayer.

Acknowledgments

Wow, how to summarize?

First of all, thank you to my massive team of beta readers, sensitivity readers, editors, proofers, and so much more. Samantha, Kerri, Gemma, Sushmita, Jennifer, and all the other quiet contributors that helped us make this book real—and deep.

Thank you for your insights, your help, and your perfection with this book.

To my readers, thank you for sticking with our Pineville family for the past nine books! It's surreal that we've made it this far and I'm grateful for every page you've read, review you've written, and email you've sent.

To my family, and my heart and soul. Love you kiddos, husband, and puppies.

Now, let's go make some more excellent books!

Also by Katie Cross

The Health and Happiness Society

Bon Bons to Yoga Pants (Lexie)

I Am Girl Power (Megan)

You'll Never Know (Rachelle)

Hear Me Roar (Bitsy)

What Was Lost (Mira)

The Health and Happiness Society Collection

Finding Anna

Coffee Shop Series

Coffee Shop Girl

Lovesick

Runaway

Fighter

Shy Girl

Wild Child

Smoke and Fire

Clean Sweep

Protect Me

About the Author

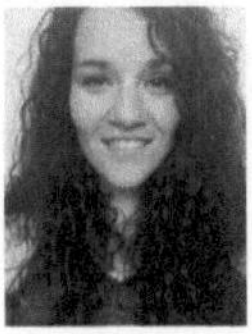

Katie Cross is ALL ABOUT writing epic love stories and wild places. Creating new books is her jam.

When she's not hiking or chasing her two littles through the Montana mountains, you can find her curled up reading a book or arguing with her husband over the best kind of sushi.

Visit her at www.katiecrossbooks.com for free short stories, extra savings on all her books (and some you can't buy on the retailers), and so much more.